I0769023

THE MONTH BEFORE CHRISTMAS

Erin Hemenway

Titles by Erin Hemenway

The Night Before Christmas

Where the Wind Howls: a collaborative anthology

Dear Mighty Queen - A Cancer Warrior's Journal

THE MONTH BEFORE CHRISTMAS

ERIN HEMENWAY

For my husband,

who helped me learn how to fly.

CHAPTER ONE

Halloween

Mary Christmas shivered in delight as the wind sliced through the crisp fall air. She loved this time of year, of course she loved this time of year. She was the Queen of Winter after all. True, she also reveled in the macabre pleasures of All Hallows Eve. Frightening parents was a favorite pastime. Overloading tiny humans with as much sugar as she could shove into greedy palms brought her a wicked amount of joy. But it was the magic of winter, not fall, that gave her a special thrill.

It meant Christmas was nearly here.

Mary smiled, a naughty and knowing smile as she sipped cocoa from a hand carved beer stein. She surveyed the empty streets like the queen she was as the soft purple hues of morning crested the skyline to banish the darkness. This neighborhood took their holidays very seriously, Halloween was no exception. The extravagant trimmings were as diverse as the houses and people. Some embracing the gory horror of monsters, some aiming for whimsical cartoons. Even the neighborhood snitch captain dressed her neutral beige rancher with quaintly colorless pumpkins and birchwood arches. *That* woman crafted her holidays like a meticulous Pinterest board… minus the personality.

Of course, as Winter Queen, Mary had the best decorations on the block by a mile, if she did say so herself. If there was a dash of magic to help her delight and frighten… well, who would know? She took her reputation as the eccentric old woman who lived in the witch house very seriously.

Her Victorian craftsman was covered in a dark swath of Halloween. Thirteen individually carved pumpkins lined the cobbled walking path. The last dregs of black candles flickered in their orange hollowed out shells. Last night an actual fire had roared beneath a behemoth cast-iron cauldron where three wraith-like witches and their brooms still danced in the wind. Bats dripped from the trees, a citrine glow-in-the-dark paint weeping from their fangs. Purple spider lights crawled over the wrought iron gate posts and twined over the leaded glass windows. Weeping angel statues covered their eyes while the neighbor's black Devon Rex cat dozed on her front porch banister, feathery tail flicking lazily at every sound. Mary grinned at her own cleverness.

It was perfection.

She waltzed up her front cobbles humming *"It's Beginning to Look a Lot Like Christmas"* while she fantasized about what magic she would weave over her home for the upcoming holidays. Her wintery power thrummed in response as she danced her way up the porch steps. With the flick of a finger, she opened her heavy oak doors. She paused to admire the fractal beauty of the star pattern glass inlaid in the wood before she took herself to bed.

A heartbeat later, the buzzing screech of power tools cut through the morning quiet like a howler monkey. Mary startled awake, limbs jolting in distressed and disoriented contractions. Her polished finger nails found her sleeping mask yanking the ruby red fabric from her face. She whipped her attention around the room just to make sure she didn't have to murder anyone in her own home. No one would be that stupid.

The metallic drone cracked through the air like a whip.

Apparently, her neighbor was that stupid.

Mary flung off the fluffy comforter in one swift swoosh. She stalked out of the room barefoot, pattering down the creamy carpeted stairs at a determined gait. She snagged her favorite fur-trimmed apple green coat, slipping her arms into the cool silk-lined sleeves. She didn't need the coat. Mary was never cold. But neighbors got weird about the darnedest things. So, she wore weather appropriate apparel whenever she was in public. Even if she forgot shoes.

Mary jerked the door open forcefully before stalking into the crisp autumn morning. The shrieking metal tool rolled through the air in abrasive concussions. She narrowed her sapphire blue eyes.

The across-the-street neighbor's eyesore of a home was a boxy monstrosity of utilitarian glass and bricks with all the imagination of an infected toenail. Inflatable monsters and ghosts lay in sagging blobs, as if someone had puked Halloween polyfibers all over his yard. An overly large red truck lurked in the driveway like a bloated rhinoceros beetle.

Unimaginative. Pretentious. Boorish.

Or maybe that was just how she felt about the man who lived there.

Robin Goodfellow—a beast of a man if there ever was one—was on his roof, power tools in hand. His mud brown hair was swept back into an absurdly small man bun. Red and black flannel clung so tightly to his arms and chest the fabric might very well burst at the seams if he breathed in too deeply. He was disassembling a garish ghoul the size of the Seattle Space Needle. He had constructed the offensive monstrosity over his front door.

Mary hoped he'd slip and fell.

She took three angry steps then stopped dead in the middle of the street. Their melding moron of a neighbor, Phyrne Nesbitt, clung to the lowest rungs of Robin's ladder. She cringed at the sight of the woman.

A bright pink silk robe slithered over her spandex sculpted silhouette. Her makeup was pancaked, her hair stiff and topographical. *Nobody is that put together before sunrise,* Mary groused. Not without a good reason. It was the sort of outfit one might wear to bed… Or right before. Depending on a woman's intentions. Mary had no intention of imagining her neighbor that way and shook her head to rid the image from her mind.

Phyrne had stuffed her feet into matching pink slippers with a disturbing amount of fluff. Perhaps she had murdered the Easter bunny and skinned it just so she could walk in the poor creatures entrails.

Mary wouldn't put it past her. Mrs. Nesbitt belonged to a number of institutions aimed at influencing and controlling the minds of their shared community. She'd joined the school board, the city's community advisory board, and of course, the neighborhood watch. Mrs. Nesbitt had a stuffy sense of propriety. It was her mission in life to see to it that her neighborhood was orderly and respectable.

Mary worked very hard to undermine her efforts.

She had an ongoing quarrel with the woman. Just last week Mary had received a politely nasty letter requesting she *'tone it down'* and *'think of the children.'* Apparently, Mary's Halloween decorations were considered ungodly.

Mary certainly hoped so.

Phyrne had followed up with a neighborhood wide letter espousing the purpose of Halloween and how one should not aim to frighten the children. All holidays, even Halloween, should be quaint, and cuddly according to Mrs. Nesbitt. Mary had promptly added six growling gargoyles and a murder of crows with glowing ruby eyes. Each now perched along the posts of her fence, glowering at any passerby.

Mary wanted to know how exactly *she* was violating the good senses of Mrs. Nesbitt with her decor. At least Mary kept All Hallows Eve to its roots, while Robin Goodfellow turned it into cheap parlor tricks. How were his ghastly ghoul and bloated balloons *not* offensive? Frankenstein's monster was still a monster, no matter how cutesy or inflatable Home Depot tried to make it.

Mary seethed, frost cracking in fractal patterns beneath her feet. Her icy blood boiled at the sight of Robin Goodfellow and Phyrne Nesbitt conspiring. She really had intended to have a pleasantly quiet Christmas this year.

CHAPTER TWO

Robin Goodfellow

Robin breathed heavily through his nose as he dismantled the gargantuan ghoul. He'd only assembled the darned thing to get his queen's attention. It had worked, but not the way he had planned. Instead of confronting him directly, Mary had doubled down on her own flawlessly creative and deeply haunting decor. Straight out of a Grimm's fairytale. Or, perhaps, her own mischievous nightmares.

They were beautiful, in their own way. Though Robin was probably the only person who would use the word beautiful to describe Mary Christmas' home. It was easily was the most popular display on the block by Halloween. In part because all the neighborhood children suspected

Mary was a real witch.

They were not entirely wrong.

She was the Queen of Winter. She had many names over the years. Today's children might know her best as Elsa, thanks to that cantankerous mouse and his board of directors. Some might call her Mrs. Claus, though she had never been married to the best of Robin's knowledge. Of all the names from all the places Mary had been, she preferred Mary Christmas…

…For the comedy.

He smiled at that, tossing another screw to the carpet of autumn leaves and green grass below. Few might think of the Queen of Winter or Mrs. Claus as funny, but she was. She was so ridiculously funny. True, her sense of humor was a little twisted. Okay, a lot twisted.

Once, she had turned an unfortunate goblin into a ceramic yard gnome for some forgotten grievance or other. He was still there, urinating in the bird bath. Come to think of it… that might very well be why she had turned him into a yard gnome in the first place.

Oh. Oh my. Was that where all the urinating yard gnomes and chubby cherubs came from? Robin sort of hoped so. He found himself chuckling out loud. He redoubled his focus on his work. He was still grinning like a fool when he heard a purposefully mousy and impossibly grating voice call to him from the foot of his ladder.

"Oh, Mr. Goodfellow," Phyrne Nesbitt crooned in a soft sing-song trill.

Hells bells. This can't be good. Robin just knew it meant trouble whenever Mrs. Nesbitt got involved. She sucked the fun right out of everything. The poor children lived in fear of her reporting back to their parents about whatever mischief they had gotten themselves into.

This morning, Mrs. Nesbitt was wearing her dressing robes, a silky pink thing that was wildly inappropriate to be talking to her unmarried neighbor in. She had cinched it tight to her waist by the sorcery of women's undergarments. Phyrne wasn't hard to look at, if Robin cared to notice. But she was also decidedly married. Miserably married, but married, none the less. Robin had a thing about married women—he avoided them. Especially if they were so unabashedly flirting with their neighbor.

"Good morning, Mrs. Nesbitt," he replied dryly.

He wasn't about to come down the ladder. Mary was probably watching. It had been a gamble to start disassembling the construction project at dawn, but he was awake.

"I wonder if I might have a word on this fine autumn morning?"

"I'm a little occupied," Robin explained. He refused to

give her his full attention. Maybe she would just go away. He was not that lucky.

"It's important, Mr. Goodfellow," Phyrne assured him.

"Of course it is," Robin growled, securing his drill and climbing down the ladder. The sooner he addressed this, the sooner she would go away. "What can I do for you, Mrs. Nesbitt?"

She pursed her lips into a constipated line. She didn't enjoy being reminded he knew exactly who her husband was. Noah was a decent enough guy. He didn't deserve a toad like Phyrne, but what were you going to do? The man was blinded by his wife's… personality.

"I wanted to thank you for being so proactive taking your Halloween decorations down," Phyrne began. "I know Halloween is special for *some* people. I just can't understand celebrating all this darkness."

"Celebrating darkness?" Robin was confused.

"It invites evil, Mr. Goodfellow," she said seriously, scratching her chunky blonde hair out of her eyes. She fluttered her lashes at him.

There were all kinds of evil in the world. This ridiculous display from his narrow minded neighbor was right up there with some of the worst villains he'd encountered. Robin was not, strictly speaking, human himself. He'd known a truly vile villain or two in his time.

Absently, he wondered what Phyrne might do if he told her who he truly was. That he was the Claus, a guardian an gift maker for children around the world. That she might call him Santa and still not believe it to be true.

He knew what his Queen would do. She would most certainly kill him for the breach of secrecy. Or, if she was feeling generous, add him to the lawn furniture as a urinating garden gnome. Robin just barely managed not to cringe.

"I think Halloween costumes and decorations are supposed to ward off the evil," Robin offered mildly, brining his thoughts back to the present moment and threat. He hooked his thumbs through his belt loops. "Confuse it so it doesn't know where to look."

"Be that as it may," Phyrne continued, "it's a despicable holiday. I'm grateful you are so efficient at bringing your home back in line with the city ordinances."

"With the what now?" Robin had only been in the neighborhood for a few years. He traveled mostly but spent summer and autumn in suburbia so he could be near his Queen. He was still new to the whole *rules* thing.

"Demonic displays are against the city ordinances," Phyrne explained. "Of course, you didn't put any up. You kept it light and encouraged children with the balloon animals."

"Balloon animals?!" Robin was deeply offended. He had carefully curated his display of ghosts, goblins, and Frankenstein's monster. Each character had been hand selected and were top of the line Spirit creations. Which wasn't saying much, but still. They were not *balloon* animals.

"Not like some people," Phyrne continued as she turned a disapproving gaze across the street. Mary Christmas' yard was just beginning to bask in sunlight, a haunting Hill House. Beautiful, in a darkly macabre way.

Then, a naughty thought bloomed to life. Perhaps he should have a bit of fun, push this woman to fawning for real. See if his queen could be made jealous. Enlisting her least favorite neighbor in his cause just might do it. He smiled broadly and slid a hand behind his neck, assuming his best "gee-shucks" posture.

"Well, ma'am," Robin said, "I wouldn't want to upset any city ordinances."

"You're a good man, Robin Goodfellow." Phyrne touched his cheek. Her hands were clammy and weirdly warm. It felt slimy to have her touch him. He went unnaturally still, the way a predator does when they felt threatened. "You know our friendly, elderly, spinster, don't you?"

Robin practically choked. If Mary Christmas ever heard

this toad of a woman call her a spinster, Phyrne would have four flat tires and that would be the least of her problems.

"I… yeah. I know her."

"And you have influence with her?"

Like an ant has influence with a boot, Robin thought crossly. Mary Christmas was his queen. Robin worked for her, no matter what the story books might say. Whatever she said was law in the land of Winter. But this insignificant woman didn't need to know that.

Robin sighed. "Some."

"Wonderful," Phyrne chirped, reluctantly taking her hand back. Robin resisted the urge to wipe her clammy sweat from his skin. "Perhaps you can wrestle her beastly demons and witches away from her then."

"I'm sorry?"

Robin glanced across the street. Mary had added gargoyles and ravens since before last nights trick-or-treating. When had she added gargoyles? At second glance, he was certain they were no ordinary gargoyles. In fact, he had the distinct impression they were watching, waiting. *Sweet Jimmy Cricket.* She had an entire clan of the stone guardians.

"I know we're not *quite* an HOA, but we still abide by their rules," Phyrne cooed.

"We do?" He swallowed a lump forming in his throat.

"We do."

"Of course we do." Robin sighed. He was regretting his decision to play Phyrne and Mary's games more and more. Maybe he'd just return to Europe, see how things were going. Maybe they'd forgotten his little mishap with the Belsnickle. Probably. Maybe. Doubtful.

"Anyway, I just wanted to thank you for being so proactive at disassembling your decorations. And, if you're open to it… I'd like to hire you to do the lighting for my house."

Robin choked. "I'm sorry?"

"I'll pay you, of course. Noah has such a bad back. I just couldn't bare it if my children didn't have a Christmas."

Phyrne was far too close again, her hand resting on Robin's bicep in some weird claim of territory. His voice strangled in his own throat as he tried to rebuke and reject this horrible little toad.

"Of course, children deserve a proper Christmas," Robin agreed before his mouth caught up with his brain. Phyrne squeezed his arm possessively. Before things could escalate and Robin got himself in any more trouble with meddlesome neighbors, he scurried up the ladder and redoubled his efforts to dismantle the ghoul.

"Ever the gentleman," Phyrne called after him with a

wink. "I look forward to what you have in mind for Christmas!"

Robin turned to tell Phyrne absolutely not, then he noticed Mary standing in the middle of the street with her hands on her hips, ice burning in her eyes.

"Son of a reindeer," he cursed and began to methodically work down a row of iron fasteners, discarding the screws off the roof.

CHAPTER THREE

Neighbors

"What in the name of all that is holy are you doing, Robin Goodfellow?" Mary demanded, digging her bare toes into his green grass. The lawn was littered with deflated Halloween decorations as her infuriating mule of a neighbor blasted his power tools. Her only satisfaction was Phyrne flinched and stumbled away from the ladder in alarm, as if she'd been caught red handed in the cookie jar. Mary rolled her eyes. She couldn't be bothered with simpering fools.

Robin stopped his drill and looked at Mary, a mocking smile on his lips. "What does it look like I'm doing, Mary Christmas?"

"Waking the whole bloody neighborhood when you

know good and well not a one of us went to bed before the cock crowed," she snapped.

"This ghoul isn't going to put itself to bed," Robin grunted. He revved the throttle on the drill, making it whine like a cat on Ritalin before he continued unspooling fasteners, adding to the pile of discarded steel in the grass.

"So help me, Robin, if you don't stop this nonsense right this minute, I will make your life miserable," Mary threatened. Careless. He could be so damned careless.

"You already do that, Mary," Robin fired back, cramming the nose of the drill into a screw. The wood and metal barked in a growling complaint as he coaxed the fastener out of the hole. He tossed the iron scrap into the grass with a leaden thud at Mary's feet.

She hopped back out of range and hissed. Iron was one of those funny materials that sometimes bothered her and sometimes didn't. A cast iron forged in flame and seasoned with oil seemed to be just fine, but the smaller less cultivated materials produced an unpleasant and severe allergic reaction. Mary started for the ladder. She would throw him off the roof if she had to.

"Oh, thank goodness," Phyrne interrupted in a raspy honeyed voice. "I was just coming to talk to you too."

"Oh Gods, really?" Mary had not had enough coffee—or gin—for this woman to knock on her door. She absolutely could not be pleasant without a pick me up or drop me down. Sleep would be best, but Robin and his damned power tools had robbed her of that. Mary growled at both of them.

"Of course, silly," Phyrne laughed. It was a grating laugh. The affectation like nails on a chalk board.

Mary was the Winter Queen, damnit. She would not be cowed by this toad of a human. Ooh! That's an idea. Maybe she could turn Phyrne into a real toad to add to her garden. *Tempting.* She stuffed the temptation back into a box where it belonged. It was simply bad manners to turn ones neighbors into toads, no matter how boorish.

"As you know, Halloween is over," Phyrne was saying.

"Halloween was *yesterday*," Mary replied hotly. She hoped her face was every bit as incredulous as she felt. All Hallows Eve had ended exactly forty-five minutes ago, for Mary at least. "We've barely tucked all the little goblins into their beds."

"I noticed that your decorations are still up. Including those… gargoyles," Phyrne said.

Mary looked at her home. The last shades of night lingered as her yard yawned awake. What had been horrific in the dark of the witching hour had settled back into extravagant adornments on an antique home. Eccentric, but not terrifying. Mary loved everything about it. Especially her gargoyles.

"Yes," was all Mary said.

"Well, I'm not sure if you are aware but they are a grave violation against the governance of this neighborhood," Phyrne went on. "As an infraction of the community guidelines, they need to be down as soon as possible."

"By five o'clock in the morning?" Mary felt her hackles rise at the flagrant order. Her skin went hot then cold, her blood boiling in simmering rage.

"I'll be sure to have the Halloween decorations down by tonight, Mrs. Nesbitt," Robin chimed in, his voice taking on an ingratiating *gee-shucks-ma'am* lilt. "Wouldn't want to upset the apple cart."

From his perch on the roof, Robin grinned at Mary. She knew he despised Phyrne as much as the next neighbor, but just to spite Mary, he'd lay it on thick. He showed his fangs in a grin—and by fangs, of course, it was a flash of perfect pearly teeth in a wolfish smile. Fools like Phyrne would fall head over heels for it. Mary was smarter than that.

"You are so thoughtful, Robin," Phyrne cooed, sucking in her stomach and adjusting her posture to emphasize her ample bosom. "And please, call me Phyrne."

Of all the things. This petulant woman. Mary clicked her tongue.

"Ma'ams." Robin revved the throttle on his power drill twice in salute and continued his obnoxious work unfastening screws from his garish billboard.

"Yes, well," Phyrne began, "as I'm sure you know, Mary. Thanksgiving is just around the corner-"

"Thanksgiving is a month away," Mary snapped.

"Twenty-one days, if you don't count today," Phyrne corrected. "Twenty-two if you count Thanksgiving itself."

"I do," Mary huffed, crossing her arms over her chest. Not because she was cold. She was never cold. But the look Robin was giving her... Was he... *enjoying* this? She was going to train the neighborhood stray cats to vomit on the hood of his truck.

"Be that as it may, it is so *soon*. And then, of course... Christmas!" Phyrne announced.

As if the Queen of Winter didn't know when one of the most famous celebrations of her season was. She wondered if Phyrne knew the true origins of Christmas. Maybe Mary would ruin it for her. No. That wasn't exactly in line with the Mrs. Claus image she worked so hard to cultivate. Though she supposed gin and gargoyles were not in line with it either. But Mary liked gin. And gargoyles.

"...we expect a bigger turn out than last year, what with the news articles and media attention. The whole neighborhood needs to participate," Phyrne continued on.

"I *always* decorate," Mary said flatly.

"Yes, well," Phyrne somehow managed to look down her nose at Mary. It was an accomplishment, considering Phyrne was lucky if she hit five foot three in six inch heels. "It is time for the hocus pocus to go away. Think of the children."

"Yes, Mary," Robin rumbled from the roof in a velvety baritone. "Think of the children."

Slowly, so slowly, Mary turned a withering gaze upon her bearish neighbor. Robin had the decency to flush and turn his attention back to his power tools.

Think of all the children who spent weeks snapping photos in their costumes in Mary's front yard. Think of the children, who hour after hour knocked on her door demanding sweets. Think of the children, who until the wee dark hours of the morning were *safe* in this neighborhood because Mary had ordered her gargoyles to chase off any hooligans bold enough to enter her territory uninvited. Even Mrs. Nesbitt's miserable little heathens had been foiled from TP-ing the elderly Mr. Crabtree's house last night by the gargoyles. It was enough to make Mary's teeth gnash.

"Yes, think of the children," Mary said menacingly. She turned on her barefooted heel, storming back into her beautiful home to plan.

"I expect to see your progress soon," Phyrne called after her with a wave of her hand, polished fingernails glistening like Pepto Bismol. "By Thanksgiving, Mary. Or we'll have to involve the authorities."

"Oh, you'll see my progress," Mary promised.

CHAPTER FOUR

Gargoyles

The street was quiet shortly after lunch. Neighbors had long since left on their way to school or work. No one noticed as Mary hefted large plastic sacks from the trunk of her sky blue vintage 1955 XK Jaguar. She wiggled her nose. With a flash of sparkle zipping around the edges, the trunk of her vehicle thunked shut.

Mary quickly made her way past the front fence and stopped at the gate. The autumn air was slowly warming as the bright sun claimed victory over another day. A slick beading of sweat coated the stones as the morning dew began to evaporate. Another crinkle of her nose and a quick glimmer dusted across the stones. The gargoyles perched on her fence were miraculously dry as bone.

"I thought we weren't allowed to use magic where people could see," Robin's voice rumbled.

Mary startled, annoyed she hadn't heard him approach. She glanced around the empty street and narrowed her eyes, determinedly returning to her work. "How fortunate for me that nobody of consequence is around."

"I see it's a pleasantries day," Robin's lips thinned, a muscle feathering in his jaw as he exhaled through his nose. Mary began sifting through her purchases. "What *are* you doing?"

"What does it look like?" Mary asked. She settled a gnomish hat with red sequins and frosted white trim on the first gargoyle's head. It shimmered in the sunlight. She fussed with it until it was lopsided, the cone flopping over at an extreme angle.

"Making enemies of neighbors," Robin said dryly.

Mary turned to face him. He was so close she could see the amusement dancing in his seawater eyes. His mouth was drawn up, hidden behind his whiskers and perfectlywhite teeth. He smiled at her before tilting his head to one side, darting his eyes toward his shoulder to suggest she look behind him.

Mary followed the gesture to find Mrs. Nesbitt standing beside her beige Suburban parked at on odd angle in front of Mary's driveway. Her lips were a putrid line of pink, cheeks hot and glowing under her pancake makeup. Her eyes blazed with murder.

"Mary Christmas!   You-whooo! Good afternoon!" Phyrne's voice set Mary's temper on edge. Just the raspy sound of it.

"I thought we were done for the day, Mrs. Nesbitt," Mary said, not bothering to hide her frustration. Not that Phyrne noticed. The woman was singularly minded when she chose to be.

"Oh, I'm sure we'll see a lot of one another over this season." Phyrne laughed.   Mary certainly hoped not. "I was just noticing your new additions to the decor this morning…"

"You said you wanted festive." Mary's smile was positively feline as she leaned casually against her gate. "I'm adding hats."

"Perhaps I wasn't as clear as I might have been," Phyrne said, her silky southern drawl slipped into a lilting smokers rasp. "Christmas is a celebration for children, family. You do have family, don't you?"

Mary bristled. She'd had a family. Once. How she ended up in suburbia, instead of ruling Winter from a throne, was another story for another time. She had work to do here though, and it would take time. So Mary let the insult slide.

"I rather like their gnomish hats, don't you? They bring a sort of Krampus charm to the season," Mary said, flourishing her wrist to gesture at her gargoyles.

"Krampus!" Phyrne exclaimed, aghast.

"Jack and Sally just wanted to see Christmas. You wouldn't want to deny them Christmas, would you?"

"Jack and Sally?"

"My gargoyles. They're the first two you come to. They do so love a good Yuletide celebration." Mary smiled again.

Phyrne seethed. "I don't know what you heard when I said that these gargoyle violate the city ordinance—"

"I quite like them," Mary continued blithely.

"They are inappropriate for the holiday and need to be removed," Phyrne croaked.

"Oh, but they're so festive now, don't you think?" Mary replied.

"Mrs. Christmas!" Phyrne huffed in exasperation. "I need you to take Halloween out of your yard and burn it. Or else I am coming back with the proper authorities."

"No need to shout. I'm old, not hard of hearing." Mary set her plastic bags down and looked deep into Phyrne's eyes. She draped manicured fingers over Phyrne's shoulder. "How are you Phyrne? Is there any trouble at home? I hear that being married can age a woman ten years into an early grave."

"You tell her!" Phyrne commanded Robin.

"Me?"

"Tell her! You tell her she has to take them down!" she fumed. "There will be consequences!"

"Mary, Phyrne says you have to take down Halloween. Or else," Robin said dryly. His blue eyes twinkled with amusement. Mary wondered what in the world he had to be pleased about. Phyrne sighed with relief as if she believed Robin had somehow solved all her problems, at least where Mary Christmas was concerned. Mary snorted.

"Thank you, Robin. I'll see you in the morning," Phyrne said, shooting him one last smile before she turned on heel and clambered into her behemoth of a vehicle.

Mary chose to claim another hat from her sack, plopping it on the head of the next gargoyle. Mrs. Nesbitt drove slowly by, giving Mary every opportunity to turn and face the beige music. Mary ignored her, intent on arranging the next cap just so. Tires bit into pavement, complaining like the shriek of a banshee as Mrs. Nesbitt sped out of sight.

"What does she mean she will see you in the morning?" Mary asked quietly.

"I'm working for her," Robin said, reluctantly. "She commissioned me to hang her Christmas lights."

"Is that what you're doing? Hanging her lights?" Mary

asked.

"Yes."

"Well, that's the way of it, isn't it?" Mary asked no one in particular.

Robin tipped his head to one side. "We watch out for each other, Mary," he said.

"Do we? As far as I can tell, you are drawing a line in the sand. Is that how one looks out for one's neighbor, *Robin?*"

"I'm just trying to help," Robin said as he lifted his hands in surrender and backed away in a dramatic show of supplication.

"I'm perfectly fine without any input from Hobgoblins or flying Reindeer," Mary muttered as he moved out of ear shot. She shot him one final glare and turned back to her task at hand.

The hats on the gargoyles was a stroke of genius, if Mary did say so herself. It did not take her long to drape each hat, cut each tag, and dangle each bell by hand. She would comply with the spirit of Mrs. Nesbitt's request, if not to the letter.

Mary was going to have to do something about her troublesome neighbor. Mary loved Christmas. Of course she did. If *she* ruined Christmas... if that despicable woman ruined Mary's favorite holiday by forcing her to be petty... If Mrs. Nesbitt forced Mary Christmas to stand her ground on Halloween, the little toad would regret it for the rest of her miserable little life.

CHAPTER FIVE

Nightmare Christmas

Robin finished tacking down a strand of white garland lights in perfectly symmetrical rows. Mrs. Nesbitt may be ruthless about her idea of holidays, but she paid well for her decorations. He was not about to turn aside paying work. Especially if it meant thumbing his nose at Mary Christmas.

Phyrne instructed Robin to make it "like magic" and then proceeded to outline the most bland directions he'd ever encountered. He'd had to scoff. Phyrne had no idea what he was *really* capable of. Magic thrummed in his veins nearly as deep as the Winter Queen. Nearly. But here he was, strangling a Birch tree with green wire and white lights because Phyrne insisted. He wasn't sure Phyrne even knew what the word magic meant. Robin sighed.

The screech of tires on pavement drew his attention to the street. Black strips of rubber fanned out behind Mrs. Nesbitt's beige SUV. It had come to a complete stop in the middle of the road. The door was flung wide, the safety chime tolling like a death knoll. Phyrne stood with her hands on hips gawking at Mary Christmas's Victorian home.

Mary had effectively turned her front yard into a Christmas nightmare. She had added a tactically garish neon green tree threaded with silver ghosts lights and glowing red eye lights. The purple bats had made their way from the fence posts into the tree as well.

Somewhere, Mary had acquired a giant plastic skeleton that had not been a part of her Halloween decoration. She'd happily dressed the bones in a red coat, red pants, the belt cinched tight around his ribs to the point of ridiculousness. She'd even pinned a tiny sequined stocking cap to his smooth plastic skull. The bony creature perched on her roof line, knee bent and a beer stein clasped in spindly fingers. *How the heck had she got a twelve foot skeleton on her roof?*

Magic, of course.

And every single gargoyle had their own Santa hat.

"Oh, dear Lord," Robin groaned. He belted his staple

gun and clambered down the ladder. Phyrne would try to make him talk to Mary again and he wanted no part of it. He needed to pack up his tools and quietly disappear before she noticed him.

He kept a wary eye on her as he shuffled through packing up his tools. Phyrne did not rant or rave, as was her typical MO. No, she deviously looked around to see if anyone was about. When Phyrne was certain she was in the clear, she stalked from the safety of her beige sedan to the wrought iron gate of Mary Christmas' gargoyles.

Phyrne quietly slipped through the gate scowling at the carved pumpkins and floating weird sisters. She tiptoed as if she were afraid to wake the dead and tacked a white notice with clear tape to Mary's front door. An officially looking red stamp was visible even at a distance.

Robin had the sinking feeling Phyrne had managed to get the city to order Mary to disassemble Halloween, effective immediately. He braced himself. If Mary caught Phyrne, he wasn't sure he wanted to be around.

Phyrne didn't ring the bell. Instead, she crept quietly off the front porch then scurried back to the gate. Her eyes darted around wildly, a neurotic glimmer of glee as she made her daring escape.

Once she crossed the boundary of the gate she turned around to glare at Mary's house once more. Her head swiveled back and forth as she considered the length of gargoyles. One by one, Phyrne went down the fence line and snatched their Santa hats off their carved stone masks.

She turned away the second she snagged the final hat with a manic expression, her cream painted cheeks flushed cranberry red with excitement. Phyrne clenched the sequins caps so tightly even from this distance Robin could see the white of her knuckles. He held perfectly still, praying she wouldn't notice him.

Quick and quiet as a rat, Phyrne raced back to her idling vehicle, the door gaping wide. She dashed the last few steps, flinging red caps into her passenger seat before throwing herself in after them and slamming the drivers door shut. Her sedan engine whined, her tires screaming as they streaked rubber in twin lines on the asphalt as she tore out of the neighborhood.

Robin blinked, unsure what to do. Had he really witnessed what he thought he had? It was tantamount to murder in his queen's mind. He wasn't entirely certain she wouldn't shoot the messenger for good measure.

He decided to keep this little bit of information to himself. He packed the last of his tools into his belt and scurried down the ladder before anyone could ask him if he'd seen a thing.

* * *

❄ ❄ ❄

Mary watched Phyrne from the parlor room window sipping her afternoon toddy from a fine porcelain teacup. Of course the wretched woman was too much of a coward to ring the bell and confront Mary directly. No, Phyrne had to hop like a toad through the gauntlet of Halloween decorations; Mary had been discretely adding dark little doodads out of spite for days.

Phyrne had just left Marys front porch, taping her notice to the door. It was the third or fourth notice this year. She turned back as if expecting to be caught, a vicious sneer on her contoured, pancake face. Mary chuckled and sipped her toddy when Phyrne bolted down the fence line and snatched the red hats of off every single gargoyle.

Before Mary could react, Phyrne had thrown herself into her vehicle and sped off so quickly she had left rubber track marks on the pavement. As if she knew she would be implicated unless she immediately disposed of the glittering evidence elsewhere. Moments later Robin high tailed it out of sight, tool box in tow as he looked over his shoulder to be sure Phyrne was gone.

"Fools," Mary said. In their haste, Robin and Phyrne had left the Nesbitt home completely unattended. Much to Mary's pure glee.

She set her teacup on the end table and made her way outside. She was careful not to attract attention as she wandered across the street at a leisurely pace. When she was perfectly certain no one was around, Mary quickened her steps and rounded the side of the house.

It took no effort at all to find the ladder tucked against the house. The beastly plastic contraption was tipped on its side, nestled in the crook of grass between the stepping stones and side paneling that hadn't quite been disposed of yet. Mary couldn't begin to fathom how just a little plastic was able to hold Robin's weight.

A wiggle of her nose, and the ladder miraculously found itself upright, leveled against the lowest trim on the Nesbitt roof. Mary easily scaled the rungs and pulled herself up. Not that it was any trouble. The Nesbitt rancher had a gentle incline on the roof, enough for runoff but not much more, unlike Mary's Victorian craftsman with its steep pitch.

She set foot on the Nesbitt roof and cringed. Rope after rope of duplicate white lights were tethered to the eaves with engineered precision. Mary shook her head and walked effortlessly along the roofline, unscrewing bulbs at random. Just enough to disrupt the circuits from connecting. When she was satisfied with her progress, Mary dusted her hands of an invisible grime and climbed back down the ladder.

Another crinkle of her nose had the ladder nestled exactly where Robin had left it. Pleased with her mischief, she found her way home. Tomorrow would be soon enough to replace her red hats.

❄ ❄ ❄

Robin could not understand it. Why on earth wouldn't the lights work? Phyrne had called to complain about his lackluster efforts just before he'd got into bed. He hurried over to inspect them, and sure enough, a patchwork of dead lines crisscrossed the roof at irregular intervals.

What in the world?

He spent the entire next day checking every single bulb by hand. At least a hundred lights had come loose between the time he'd tacked them down and when Mrs. Nesbitt had plugged them in. Even with his winter blood, his fingers had started to turn purple.

As the sun began to set and he was *finally* able to climb down. He settled the ladder back in its place, ready for the stew that had been slow cooking in his kitchen since morning, but then he spotted his queen.

Mary was barefoot, though the weather was starting to turn and neighbors would soon ask questions. Her lavender camisole and bohemian pants wholly unsuitable in this weather for any pretense of being human. She was fussing with a bag, wiping clean each gargoyle by hand.

As soon as she spotted him, she beckoned for him to join her. Robin sighed through his nose and hustled across the road. He tugged his coat tighter around his shoulders, approaching cautiously as he blew on his chilled fingers. Mary took a long time looking him up and down, a neutral expression on her face.

"Yes, my queen?"

"Your hands are blue," she said.

He examined his hands and they had indeed turned a purplish blue. He narrowed his eyes at her, tilting his head to one side in an unspoken question. She lifted her chin in defiance, daring him to question her. He sighed and stuffed them in this pockets. "Did you need something?"

"I noticed that the lights were not up to your usual professional touch at the Nesbitt house. Trouble in bland-land?"

Robin raised an eyebrow. Her tone was too indifferent, too innocent. She blinked at him while she waited, batting her eye lashes in guileless fashion. *Of course she did,* he grumbled.

"At least one hundred lights seemed to have come loose. They had to be found one by one and refastened," he said carefully.

"How bothersome," Mary replied as she plopped another sequined hat on the next gargoyle.

"Bothersome," Robin agreed with an irritated growl. "That's a word for it."

Mary turned her icy blue gaze on him. "Since you are so inclined to choose sides, I wonder if you might be our go between?"

"My queen?"

"You must know I have no intention of speaking directly to that wretch unless I absolutely have to," Mary explained. "You seem like a fine intermediary."

"I don't think I'd like to get involved," Robin hedged. "If that's all right by you."

"Involved? You, my merry old elf, jumped right into the thick of it when you agreed to be her personal lineman."

"I did no—"

"As such, you, my kinsman, can inform the beastly little toad I will be retaining my All Hallows decor as long as I fancy!" Robin had no intention of telling Phyrne any such thing. Mary was so heated he thought it best not to interrupt to tell *her* that, so he stayed quiet.

"You tell her she may post as many Pinterest scraps of primary school crafts on my door as she pleases. I will not be cowed by small minded flapdoodles!"

"You know what Pinterest is?"

"Robin Goodfellow!"

Robin had to fight to keep from laughing, which would not do either of them any favors at this exact moment. Instead, he leaned closer to murmur gently in her ear. "You do know one of you is a queen, yes? An ancient and powerful mistress of winter and wonder." Robin stepped back and looked down at Mary. Her eyes snapped with surprise. He took the opportunity to offer her a sincere smile. "Don't you find all of this a bit petty, even for you?"

Mary crossed her arms over her chest. "She started it."

"I know how much the Yule season means to you," Robin said.

"You think this is how I imagined spending my winter?" Mary spun away from him and jammed the final hat down on the gargoyles bald head so firmly the seams split. She huffed a breath of air and wiggled her nose. The threads reformed as if it had never happened.

"It is beneath you," Robin said.

"So? If it's war she wants, then it is war she will get." Mary turned to face him, finished with decorating her stone guardians. She lifted her chin in challenge.

"Yes, my queen." Robin bent his head in supplication.

"Stop calling me that where the neighbors can hear you," she snapped. Mary took her discarded bags from the craft store and stormed back toward her house. Robin waited for her to slam the door and turn on her Halloween lights.

"Yes, my queen."

❄ ❄ ❄

This was not what Mary had envisioned for Christmas this year. The whole ordeal was rapidly dissolving from friendly rivalry into all out war. She wasn't sure she had the stomach for it. Of course she had the stomach for it. She would not be cowed by small minded bootlickers. She'd seen herself to bed with a smidgen of tea and a night cap and that was that.

Mary awoke to the sounds of scratching. It wasn't uncommon in her old rickety house to hear creaks and groans. The occasional whomp-bang from the old oil boiler as it turned over had become a familiar soothing song.

This grating sound was as jarring as it was alarming. She tore the red silk sleep mask from her eyes. She tilted her head to one side, attentively listening. It could be the neighbors Devon Rex cat. For some reason, the feline was smitten with Mary's banister.

Occasionally, the creature would haul dead animals to Mary's door and scratch at the paneling until Mary came to acknowledge the gift with a saucer of cream. She didn't mind rodents as a rule but when they started nibbling and nesting in her walls, she had a problem. So, Mary welcomed the neighbor cats night time visits and morbid gifts.

A long brittle sound, like a shovel scraping snow away from a walkway, crawled through the quiet of the night. Something heavy was being dragged across pavement. And the only thing in her yard that could make that sound… Well there were a lot of things. The cauldron was still there to taunt Mrs. Nesbitt.

Mary had a variety of gnomes and frog stone statues in her yard year round. Some of them she had purchased at the local thrift to keep the others company. Some of them had once been a person or elf who had made her cross for one reason or another and now they adorned her lawn.

Those were the days. When she could turn any old fool into an ice sculpture or marble statue. Now she was resigned to petulant wars with neighbors over holiday ornaments.

Mary sat up in bed.

The gargoyles.

While the new sequined hats may have been cemented in with a dash of magic, the gargoyles themselves were simply ornamental. They had not been mortared into place or spelled into protection because who would steal a whole gargoyle? It was just bad manners to steal a gargoyle. They took offense to such things.

She had honestly only added them to her display when a strongly worded letter had arrived signed by the Neighborhood Snitch Captain in the early weeks leading up to Halloween. The decorations were too scary for the "children" and needed to be "toned down."

Mary had promptly added thirteen gargoyles for spite.

The woman was lucky *all* Mary had done was add gargoyles to her fence posts. If she really wanted to be nasty, she'd have turned her home into a Krampus Halloween, completely with horned demons stealing and eating children from their beds. She had briefly considered borrowing Mrs. Nesbitt's nasty little hooligans for the centerpiece. Better angels had prevailed and she settled for stone gargoyles decidedly not made from neighborhood children who bothered her.

Another lingering metallic scrape dragged down the pavement.

"Oh, for heaven's sake," Mary cried out in exasperation.

She tossed aside her comforter and stalked straight down the stairs and out into the night. She didn't bother with human formalities like a coat and boots this time. Her winter blood would do just fine to keep her comfortable. She expected to catch whoever was stealing her precious new additions red handed. The rules be damned. They would join her ever growing gnome collection.

She burst through her front door with a bang, the heavy oak swaying wildly until it thumped against her wall and rattled the glass. Mary stood on the porch flicking her gaze left and right. The street was quiet, a crisp breeze playing with the periwinkle silk of her pajama bottoms. Wisps of her snowy hair danced around her face. She stalked further down the steps to get a better look around.

Nothing appeared out of place. Her cauldron and the three sisters were where she had left them. Her pumpkins, spelled to not rot, flickered their candlelight down the walk way. She couldn't see the gargoyles from where she stood but six languid strides and she had exited her front gate. Jack and Sally sat where they belonged, all her xenomorphs exactly where she left them. Their sweet and sparkling red hats were all present and accounted for.

Mary raised her eyes to look around the neighborhood. It was quiet. She turned to go back into her home and froze. There on her roof, the high-density polyethylene skeleton... the one she had spent so much time lovingly dressing up like Santa. The gleaming bones and glowing eyes little children had squealed over, tugging on their parent's arms to look up on afternoon walks. The only element in her entire yard she had purchased for a hefty sum from the hardware store. The twelve-foot skeleton was gone.

Someone had been in Mary's yard. Someone had stolen Mary's Santa hats in broad daylight. Someone had stolen her skeleton. And Mary knew exactly who to blame.

Mrs. Nesbitt's house was illuminated with the ever growing shades of white. The plainness of it grated Mary's nerves. Other houses had slowly begun the process of packing in Halloween and unboxing Christmas too, but none had gotten nearly as far as Phyrne Nesbitt, thanks to Robin Goodfellow and his traitorous carpentry skills.

Mary just knew it was this tasteless woman who had stolen her precious skeleton. She was certain of it in her bones. Who else could it be? Because it was that rotten toad who had written the strongly worded letter to the *entire* neighborhood about the skeleton the day Mary installed it.

The light in Phyrne's garage winked out, and the muffled thunk of a door being dead bolted puffed against the quiet of the night. The timing was just too coincidental. Phyrne was clearly awake and making every effort to go unnoticed.

Mary had had about enough.

It was time to show this neighborhood bully just who was Queen. Mary stalked into the middle of the street, barefoot, her silky nightclothes whispering over her skin. Frost cracked under her feet where she stepped. She knelt at the edge of Phyrne's manicured grass, touching one icy finger to the blades.

Mrs. Nesbitt's award winning yard transfigured into a carpet of barren sickly husks, the green blades withered and cracked into sallow shards of grass. A howling winter wind whipped through the neighborhood tearing autumn leaves from branches and scattering them across manicured lawns.

"And to all, a good night," Mary growled.

CHAPTER SIX

Neighorhood Watch

Early that morning, Phyrne discovered her lawn had been vandalized. The vibrant blades of green had withered to oblivion during the night. A wicked and untimely case of frost had wiped out the lawn. And *only* the lawn. No other house on the block had suffered any sort of early winter ailment.

Mrs. Nesbitt promptly called a Neighborhood Watch meeting for six o'clock sharp at her home.

Phyrne ushered neighbors into her oversized living room. The Nesbitts' spacious five bedroom three bath rancher had been built sometime in the 1970s. It had pink plush carpeting and white washed walls. Phyrne had done very little to modernize, the original design was holding on with its teeth.

People perched on large cream colored couches angled in an L-pattern, each end separated by oakwood and glass side tables. Every possible spare surface was covered in a glass knickknack of some kind, and Robin was concerned he'd break something if he sneezed wrong.

He nestled in the comfortable brown leather chair stuffed in a corner near the fireplace as far from any delicate adornments as he could manage. He could watch the entire show from this angle of the room. As best as Robin could tell, Mary Christmas had been excluded from the little S.O.S. meeting. Mary might flatten the house with a tornado if she learned where everyone was.

His neighbors shuffled about, sampling hor d'oeuvres and burnt cookies, selecting fruit or veggies and piling them on flimsy paper plates. They mingled and siphoned off into familiar groups. Some claimed the available real estate of the oversized couches while others queued along walls and windows. It felt more like an open house than an emergency neighborhood watch meeting.

Robin liked his neighbors for the most part. Nearly all of them came to these meetings when they could. Families, single dwellers, and renters alike. The neighborhood had struggled to feel as cohesive as it had a decade ago, as new families came and went. The weekly Watch meetings offered a safe place to get to know one another—even if they were held at Phyrne's house.

"I am so glad you could all make it," Phyrne trilled, raising her sickly sweet voice over the din of conversation. Slowly the room gave her their attention.

"What seems to be the issue?" Cyrus Crabtree asked. His black and silver hair hung in two thick braids over his warm green flannel shirt. He was trying desperately to not break a tooth on one of Phyrne's cookies. After several attempts, Cyrus gave up on the cement like cookie, contenting himself to a cheese stick and sipping on whatever concoction was in the punch bowl. Robin had taken one whiff and left it clear alone.

"Well, as you know Thanksgiving is just around the corner." Phyrne clapped two hands together as if she could barely contain herself. She was in a finely pressed power suit that emphasized her generous proportions. Beige, of course. Her hair was slicked back into a tight bun, the extreme pressure acting as a do-it-yourself facelift. Robin chuckled, crumbling the brittle cookie to dust on his plate.

"Yeah, we noticed," a male voice from the back of the room groused.

"And you're already neck deep in Christmas," the woman to Phyrne's right grumbled. She'd have to be careful, Robin observed, or she would lose control of the group.

Everyone participated in the friendly festive decorating spectacular, but not all of them loved it. Many of them had been suckered into an unspoken agreement that had turned into a mandatory tradition. Unless they were as old as Mary, very few knew anything about the rule when they were looking for new homes. Some just never put up a fuss and went with the flow. All of them took their responsibility very seriously.

"People expect our neighborhood to be a complete wonderland transformation by Black Friday. So why wouldn't I make the effort to transform from the drab dreary fall into Christmas at the earliest possible measure?" Phyrne huffed a laugh.

"I don't see what that has to do with all of us," Selena Ortiz commented. The frazzled mother had her six-year-old Magdelena coloring contentedly in her lap. Selena would clearly rather not be here. The six-year-old would make an excellent reason to vacate the premises if she needed one. Robin wondered where her other children might be. There were three, two boys in addition to the girl if memory served him.

"Well, I'm sure some of you have noticed that our resident Luddite has not yet taken down her Halloween decorations. And some of them..." Phyrne shuddered, as though the mere memory was just too much to bear. "Those hideous stone monsters for example—"

"Gargoyles!" a young girl with pink hair, glitter box framed glasses, and a *Princess of Power* T-shirt chimed in. Her mother, who looked more like an older sister in a different fandom shirt and ruby red glasses, sat beside her.

Robin took a moment to recall their names. Jade and Sandra Griffith. Sandra was a math teacher at the high school and sometimes coached various sports to pick up extra income. It left Jade to her own devices more often than not but she was a good kid. Jade was always on Robin's nice list. Sandra squeezed her daughter's knee. The girl sat forward determined to be heard.

"They are gargoyles, not stone monsters. I think the Santa hats are super cute."

"I—" Phyrne seemed at a loss on how to respond to that. Someone liked Mary's decorations. She finally managed to compose herself and look away from the girl dismissively as she addressed the adults in the room. "Well, they are against HOA ordinance I'm afraid. Sadly, the city is not willing to press things further. I called this meeting to encourage the rest of you to begin your own holiday transformations so we might encourage our little Luddite to—"

"Mommy, what does Luddite mean?" Magdelena asked without looking up from her coloring. Phyrne shot Selena a look as she murmured to her daughter in Spanish. Robin choked on his laugh.

"Sorry I'm late."

Everyone in the room turned their attention to find Mary Christmas holding a plate laden with cookies. A delicate buttery scent wafted into the room as if carried on a phantom breeze. Everyone inhaled and sighed with pleasure. Mary was famous for her cookies.

"I wanted to make sure these were ready to share," Mary continued as she set the platter in the center of the coffee table, covering Phyrne's burnt crispy cookies without so much as an excuse me.

Mary had two dozen golden short bread cups filled with chocolate mouse and topped with perfectly rosy strawberries. The tiniest dollop of cream cheese frosting piped around the berry tips competed the perfectly festive cookie. They looked like itty bitty edible Santa hats.

Mary wasn't petty. Not at all.

Phyrne looked like she'd swallowed a toad. "We were just discussing some community business," she bristled.

People immediately began snatching greedy handfuls of Mary's cookies. She sighed in smug satisfaction. Her smile was radiant as a winter snow under a full moon. Robin pounced on a cookie of his own before they all disappeared.

"Excellent. My community alert must have been lost in mail. That pesky Neighbors website confounds me. I am, after all, a Luddite," Mary said cooly. "An oversight, I'm sure. I'm glad I could make it, notifications or not."

She slipped one hip onto the couch arm next to Cyrus, crossing one leg over the other and hooking slim fingers over her knee. Cyrus smiled warmly at her and chewed thoughtfully on his new buttery cookie. She grinned back as he melted into his seat with a sigh. Mary turned her victorious gaze to Phyrne expectantly. She knew what the meeting was about. Robin wondered if Phyrne knew she knew.

"I'm sure," Phyrne seethed.

"We were discussing the annual holiday decorations," Robin cut in, attempting to diffuse the tension. He managed not to flinch when both women redirected their heated stares away from one another and toward him. Mary's lips twitched, amusement or annoyance it was hard to say. Phyrne was most definitely annoyed, her plan to sway the community to her cause had been resoundingly thwarted.

"Yes, we were," Phyrne commented. "We were also discussing how we are to meet the expectations of our community. Standards must be upheld."

"Standards?" Mary asked. "I didn't know we had standards." She pulled a packet from her pocket, a small bound booklet with the community bylines. It was weathered, the pages curling at the edges. Mary made a show of licking her finger and thumbing through. She settled reading glasses on her nose. Robin knew she had no need of them. She wore them around her neck for the theatrics it gave her. It was probably just plain sugar glass Mary spun along with her cookies.

"Yes, I see. Each home shall decorate from time to time for holidays as appropriate. The homeowner is responsible for any costs incurred and thereby may decorate to their own desired fullness." Mary paused, lowering her glasses just enough to peer over them at Phyrne. "To their own desired fullness."

"Your Halloween decorations are an abomination," Phyrne hissed. "They will bring down the entire tone of the upcoming holidays. It will ruin Christmas."

"Oh have a cookie, Phyrne," Mary puffed. "Stop baking in the wrong kitchen."

The overcrowded room felt warm, people whipping their heads back and forth in a volley. Some stuffed more of Mary's cookies into their mouths and pockets. Others, the ones who privately agreed with Phyrne, managed to choke down blackened bits of ginger and sugar from Phyrne's plate of cookies.

Battle lines were being drawn in realtime.

"Perhaps we can make a proposal, something that we can all agree to?" Robin interjected again. His lips curled into a soothing smile that would make Mary see red. It never failed to work on the crowd though. The room considered Robin's suggestion.

Mary narrowed her eyes at him. He had already started decorating his own home in the same white light style as Phyrne. It was a counter to Mary's gingerbread wonderland and whimsical, if macabre, Halloween. He'd planned the symmetrical aesthetic just to spite Mary, not exactly align with Phyrne. It had just worked out so spectacularly well.

"I propose for all who wish to participate this year may do so, in whatever manner they see fit. We can vote as a community on who has the best display. Whoever wins gets to set the rules for next year," Mary said.

"What if we can't afford new decorations every year?" Selena asked. Several people were nodding and murmuring their agreement.

Robin knew this was the trouble with an HOA. If they set a rule and neighbors couldn't follow it due to cost or other obstacles, it was grounds to force the neighbor to move out. He *hated* all HOA's for that. It was ruthless, and he wouldn't allow it. Not while he was here.

"An addendum then. If you just want to participate in the holiday for fun, and not the competition, you may do so to the best of your abilities, regardless of aesthetics," Robin concluded.

"Regardless of aesthetics?" Phyrne was horrified.

"Storing decoctions for only a few weeks a year or discarding and buying new every season is cost prohibitive for most of us," Cyrus said, to no one in particular, popping another cookie into his mouth. How had he snagged so many?

"Not to mention they are terrible for the environment," Sandra said through a mouthful of shortbread. "We really should be reusing old materials instead of buying new every year."

"How is that Christmas!" Phyrne demanded. "It isn't Christmas if it isn't traditional. What Mary is doing mocks—"

"There are eleven different holidays between now and the new year," Jade interrupted.

"I beg your pardon?" Phyrne demanded in an icy tone.

Robin shot her a sharp look. He liked the girl and her mother. Sandra nodded at her daughter encouragingly when all the adult heads swiveled to hear her speak. Jade squared her shoulders and lifted her chin to look Phyrne dead in the eye.

"Christmas may be the most recognized," Jade continued. "but it's not the only one. Traditions might be super different from house to house, even on the same block. They all deserve to be celebrated."

Phyrne's jaw dropped open in protest. Robin immediately began to calculate how best to reward the girl this Christmas.

"Why don't we simply celebrate our community? Let everyone decorate however they wish?" Mary asked innocently, turning a radiant smile on the room.

"However they wish?" Phyrne was dismayed. Mary beamed with delight.

"An excellent idea," Selena cut in, standing to her feet with her daughter on her hip. "We allow people to decorate however they want. Then, at the end of the season we will vote on the best house. Whoever wins sets the theme for next year. Exceptions will be made for whoever doesn't wish to participate or can't afford to. All in favor?"

She raised one hand in the air and looked around the room, daring any of them to challenge her. Selena liked Mary, though Robin wasn't sure Mary even knew who she was. Robin liked Selena and her numerous family members. They were good people.

"Aye," the sentiment echoed through the room as people reluctantly or exuberantly affirmed the proposal. Phyrne pouted unhappily. She had lost. Mary had won the round.

"Thank you, Selena," Mary said. "I believe this is a fair and honest proposal. One we can all get behind. I say aye."

Robin knew she was only goading Phyrne at this point. Christmas was Mary's favorite holiday of the year. She was only including Halloween in her Christmas decorations to spite their interfering neighbor. If Phyrne would shut up for a half a minute, Mary might let it go.

Maybe.

Possibly.

Unlikely.

Phyrne scowled.

"This meeting is adjourned," she snapped and stalked out of the room.

❅ ❅ ❅

Mary crossed the street at a gleeful gait. She would *not* be bested by small minded dictators. She would *not* sink to their level and deprive herself of her most beloved holiday. Christmas would come to the Christmas house, and by heaven, hers would be the best house on the block. To do that, Mary would have to let go of her own petty tendency toward spite. Even so, she stubbornly wanted one more night with Halloween.

"Decking the halls so soon?" Robin purred.

She'd known he would follow her out of the meeting. Just like she knew he was the one to coax the little coup d'état out of the community and turn it into a competition. Robin was a very competitive man. Mary wasn't about to let him get the best of her.

"If I must," Mary sighed. She had snapped her fingers as soon as she'd set foot in her garden. Yards and yards of ribbons appeared. Fat red ribbons trimmed in gold. Each length carefully woven through her fence line, twining around her gargoyles fearsome figures. She had decided Jack and Sally would become permanent installations.

"I thought we ought to set some parameters for ourselves," Robin offered mildly, eyeing the gargoyles warily.

"Oh?" Mary asked in an innocent tone she knew would irritate him. She didn't want him to know there was more to her gargoyles than stone. He turned his gaze from the sculptures and narrowed his eyes at her. Mary blinked wide like a doe.

"It isn't fair, using our particular gifts against the lot of them," Robin said cautiously, as he waved a vague hand behind him, encompassing the entire neighborhood with a sweeping gesture. "I think you and I should agree to no magic."

"No magic?" Mary was aghast, her voice spiked into a strained octave. Asking Mary to go without magic was like asking her not to breathe. Of course she didn't use it for every little thing. Neither did Robin, as far as she knew. But you don't inspire the world into believing in Santa and Mrs. Claus without a touch of magic here and again.

"No magic," Robin repeated. "We do this the old fashioned way."

"Magic *is* the old fashioned way," Mary argued stubbornly. "I was decorating trees and spinning snow into chubby frosted men long before this lot could even say Christmas."

She sighed and turned to find Robin with his arms folded across his massive chest. He was truly a remarkable man. And, despite years of brutal winters, he was still merry, still kind. At least to everyone else. He hadn't been pleasant to her since she'd tricked him into taking up the mantle of the Claus.

And *that* had been a very long time ago.

"Fine," Mary said crisply.

"No magic to decorate. No using our gifts to influence the neighbors one way or the other," Robin carefully outlined his desired intentions.

"I would never use magic to directly influence our neighbors," Mary pooh-poohed dismissively. He leveled her with a heavy appraising stare. Mary threw up her arms in exasperation. "I can't help it if they gobbled down cookies without asking what was in them!" Robin tilted his head with raised his eyebrows, patiently waiting for her to agree to the full extent.

"Yes, alright!" Mary waved her hands as if swatting away an insect that had been bothering her. "I won't use my magic to decorate my home or influence any of the neighbors to choose me."

Robin extended his hand as though he wanted to shake on it.

"Oh for heavens sake," Mary complained. But she clasped his hand in agreement. A firm shake and a zip of electricity buzzed between the two of them as the bargain was made. Mary snatched back her hand, shaking off the lingering sting in her fingers.

"Goodnight, my queen," Robin said.

"Don't call me that," Mary hissed. "Someone might hear you."

Robin dropped his voice to a conspiratorial purr. "Yes, my queen."

She damned near blasted him into a statue right then and there in the middle of the street. She could use another gremlin for her garden. He'd make a delightful cherubic gnome given his bone structure and occupation. Or a toad. She had a delightfully large collection of stone toads that had once been princes... She sighed, quite proud of herself for her restraint as Robin laughed himself all the way back to his front door.

CHAPTER SEVEN

Cauldron Boil and Bubble

One more night. She would leave Halloween exactly where it was for one more night. Christmas could come tomorrow. She marched inside, brewed a strong drought of herbal tea, then collapsed into her favorite over-stuffed chair with a new book.

It was morning when Mary realized she had spent the entire night reading. She'd been so caught up in the book she hadn't even realized she'd drifted off to dreamland. The midmorning light and chirping birds had roused her from sleep.

She'd stumbled through her morning routine in a daze. After a hurried spell in the shower, she was clean and pink from the hot water. She tugged on a pair of crisply folded blue jeans and paired it with a loose purple bohemian blouse that tapered at her wrists.

Freshly washed, caffeinated, and dressed for a busy day of labor, Mary fixed her attention on the exterior of her home. Halloween was looking a little jaded in the grey autumn light. Leaves and decorations had started to sag from the cold. A dismal example of post Halloween revelry. She would have to take it all down and start over.

Without any magic, she shuddered. Well, there wasn't any time to waste.

Mary spent the remainder of her morning boxing up dark and whimsical trinkets that had turned her Victorian home gothic. They were lovingly stored in tins and bins for the following year. She worked through the morning, unstringing spiders and dismantling ghosts. She had come to terms that petty wasn't going to win her any trophies.

And she would *win* that metaphorical neighborhood trophy.

She had just dragged her ladder out of her garage to reach her rafters when she heard an unfamiliar car turn down the street. It crept to a stop just beyond her driveway. Mary turned to greet the stranger and was surprised to find a police cruiser idling.

"Afternoon, ma'am," said a tall man in hunter green slacks and matching winter jacket. A mustard yellow star was stitched over his heart, the words "Skagit Valley Sheriff" in bold stitches beneath it. Whoever had designed the County Sheriff uniforms needed to be smacked. Maybe tarred and feathered, just for emphasis. Hunter green and mustard yellow? Mary shuddered.

"Officer," she called in greeting, nodding in his direction.

"Sergeant Ellis, ma'am. This your home?"

"I'm standing in front of it, am I not?" Mary replied tartly.

"Yes, ma'am." He left his vehicle idle and stepped onto the curb beside her. She could just hear the chatter on his radio as the door whomped shut. "I see you're decorating for the holiday."

"Every year," Mary confirmed. She didn't want to think about how many years it had been. A lot. But in this city, on this block... it had still been too many to count.

"I have to ask," he began. "You planning on taking down the gargoyles?"

Mary blinked and turned to look at her gargoyles. She had replaced the stolen Santa hats the very next day, adding flashy sequins of silver and red to their trim. She had bespelled them securely into place before her no-magic agreement. The gremlin responsible for the theft would have to steal the whole damned gargoyle this time.

She would love to see Phyrne try it.

Even so, Mary was baffled what crime her gargoyles and their sequins could possibly have committed. She certainly hadn't crossed any civil laws. That she knew of.

"I'm sorry?" she asked.

"There have been complaints," the officer hedged, gently.

"Complaints you say?"

"Yes, ma'am. The gargoyles are not exactly in line with the city code of ethics." He dug his booted toe into the wild grass that had escaped her lawn in the late fall. Mary hadn't bothered trimming it back since it was good for the spiders and bees. Her infrequently kept lawn was a greater violation of "city codes" than the gargoyles. Of that, Mary was certain.

Phyrne had complained last spring.

"The city code of *ethics*?" Mary echoed as neutrally as she could manage.

"Yes, ma'am."

She was fairly certain there was no such thing. Not when it came to holiday décor. She'd seen plenty a house with questionable tastes.

Just look at Phyrne's crime against minimalism.

Mary studied the officer from top to toes and back again. She squinted to examine his name more carefully before she looked down her nose at him. A feat of fortitude considering he was a good foot taller than she was.

"I see. Officer Ellis, is it?"

"*Sergeant* Ellis," he corrected her. "Yes ma'am."

"No relation to Phyrne Ellis-Nesbitt, I trust," Mary said sweetly.

Sergeant Ellis had the decency to flush like a strawberry. "A cousin, ma'am."

"I see," she said, her sapphire eyes glittering with frost.

A sudden and biting wind whipped down the block with gale force. Sergeant Ellis had to restrain his hat, though Mary was entirely unbothered. She wasn't about to argue with an officer of the law, however. It was not worth the trouble it would cause. She knew who had complained. It was a call that deserved an equally measured retaliation.

Phyrne didn't know what she was getting herself into.

"There have been complaints," he said again.

"Yes, you said that already," Mary replied tartly.

"About light pollution as well," he said.

Mary hadn't even begun to string lights. Not like Robin, whose symmetrical eye sore gleamed as soon as the sun went dark. Or Mrs. Nesbitt's equally tiresome luminations blazing with white phosphorescence at 5:02 pm exactly.

Mary clicked her tongue. "Light pollution?"

"Yes, ma'am. We know this neighborhood becomes the beacon of Christmas for this town come the day after

Thanksgiving, but until then… We gotta make sure we ain't keeping no one up at night."

"Certainly not," Mary agreed. She was tempted to put a lighthouse on the roof just to see who blinked first. Perhaps a trip to the hardware store *was* in order. She'd buy every light fixture in stock. Just see if she didn't. "Would you like a cookie, Sergeant?"

Seemingly out of nowhere, Mary produced a golden tin of cookies. She opened the lid and revealed sugar dusted buttery perfection shimmering in the golden aura of the tin. Sergeant Ellis reached in and popped a cookie in his mouth.

"Thank you, ma'am" he said with a mouthful. "You enjoy your holidays."

"I'll see to it, Officer. Thank you for your time." Mary grinned as he climbed back into his vehicle. He tipped his hat to her as he put his vehicle in drive and moseyed onwards.

Mary turned her back on her own home to face Mrs. Nesbitt's mayonnaise salad of a home. Perhaps Mary should simply talk to Phyrne, be the bigger person.

Then an earsplitting banshee cry of a power saw blade whip-cracked through the calm afternoon air.

In the Nesbitt garage.

And Robin was its master.

She knew he had been hired to do their decorating work in the past. She remembered him saying he would be doing it again this year. He was going to accost her with his own bulbous inflatable decorations *and* whatever nonsense that lifeless bore of woman concocted.

A bargain was a bargain. She had agreed she would not use magic to decorate for their community. Mary ground her teeth. *Just breathe.* It would all be worth it when she won.

She picked up an A-frame ladder from the side of her house, stacking it under the tree where she had suspended the three witches and their brooms. She'd been reluctant to bring them down, but her visit from the sergeant had tipped the balance. Phyrne was going to become a problem if Mary didn't at least *pretend* to comply. Halloween needed to come down.

Or be reborn.

A part of her wondered if perhaps she could repurpose her witches into something. Maybe angels. Or the ghosts of Christmas. Keep to the spirit of the rules while continuing to thumb her nose at Phyrne. And Robin. Stars above how she was angry with them both.

Mary unhooked the witches red gauzy frames and set them on the grass. Their brooms thunked down a moment later. She stacked all of it inside the giant cauldron.

The large bronze base and silver lined bowl had belonged to her predecessor, the last Queen of Winter. It was a great shimmering beast of a pot the size of large shrubbery. It's face was carved with delicate etchings, old magic runes to keep the cauldron from tarnishing. Mary had used it to make all manner of things over the centuries. It had been well loved and well cared for. It was a shame to shove it back in the basement.

How often did one get to use an authentic ancient cauldron?

Then, Mary had a splendid idea. Abandoning the gauzy witches and their brooms, she went on the hunt for baubles. Fat glassy baubles in reds and greens and golds covered in shimmering sparkles for good measure. She planned to leave the witches hats in the bowl of the cauldron as a base platform. But the baubles… oh yes, Mary was pleased as punch with the cleverness of it all.

In the end, Mary did not have enough globed ornaments in her own collection to achieve her desired effect. She'd had to run to the craft store again. It was her third trip this week and they'd recognized her on sight, greeting her as though she were any other grandmother crafting for her grand babies. When Mary cleaned them out of ornaments, they hadn't even batted an eye.

Heaven bless craft store women.

Mary's vintage blue Jaguar was barely large enough to contain her purchases. She left the doors flung open as she hauled box after box onto her lawn. Only a few neighbors stopped to watch, shaking their heads and continuing on their afternoon walks as she went about her business. Mary didn't have time for them anyway.

She started with the glass orbs the size of basketballs and gently stacked the globed glass on top of the witches hats. She mixed colors at random intervals until the delicate orbs crested the lip of the cauldron. She used a clay based putty to stick a waterfall of glass balls in wild shades of Christmas down the shimmering bronze and silver shoulders. The clay would easily be removed come spring and cause no damage to her precious runes.

"Cauldron bubbles?" a male voice asked from her gate. It was the mailman, his blue winter uniform buttoned up to his chin. He grinned broadly, white teeth shining against his dark brown skin.

Mary smiled back. "I can't tell you how happy I am that someone on this street appreciates me, Omar," she said, pausing in her work to meet Omar at the gate and receive her mail by hand.

"I was sad to see you were pulling down Halloween so soon," Omar said with a tip of his hat. "Mr. Crabtree agreed with me when I delivered his post."

"I assure you gentleman, this is merely a seasonal transition," Mary said with a smile, accepting a handful of envelopes from him. "I think I'll put them up sooner next year."

The day after summer solstice would do nicely if Mary was still feeling petty by then.

"Your street is the best street in town from October to New Year's. Your house in particular..." Omar's grin widened. "Your house is always my favorite."

"You may be on the very best good list this year, kind sir," Mary told him with real enthusiasm for the first time in days.

"You have a good afternoon, Miss Christmas." Omar tipped his hat again, a knowing twinkle in his eye. Maybe he suspected her true name. Maybe he just enjoyed her decorations. Either way, she felt a confidence and joy she hadn't felt since that wretched Mrs. Nesbitt had left her ridiculous notice on Mary's door.

"Uh... Mary?" Omar had returned. His voices was thin, his jaw tight and his eyes anxious. He wrapped both gloved hands around the brass tipped iron posts of her gate.

"Yes, Omar? What can I do for you?"

"Don't tell Miss Phyrne I like your house better. She leaves a mighty fine tip in the mailbox every Christmas morning. If she thinks I don't like her decorations best..." Omar trailed off, his lips thinning into a frustrated grimace.

Mary knew. Phyrne was as petty as Mary could be. More so, apparently, if she was low enough to withhold a Christmas gift like it was a game of cat and mouse.

"Your secret is safe with me," Mary assured him with a gentle squeeze of his hand.

Omar sighed with relief. "My family counts on that little bonus to make up the gap for Christmas gifts."

"You have my word," Mary vowed. She offered him a radiant smile as he shuffled away to deliver the rest of his packages. Mary made a mental vow to make certain Omar got everything on his Christmas list this year. She spent the rest of her day perfecting her cauldron bubbles just for him.

CHAPTER EIGHT

Cider House Rules

Robin hadn't intended to get in an all out feud with the Queen of Winter. It was by no means a smart move on his part. They had come to an agreement about their little decorating feud. No magic, and the neighbors would all make the final call together on who had the best display.

But she couldn't stop meddling. He knew beyond any shadow of a doubt Mary was the one to unscrew the light bulbs. She'd practically bragged about it. Not to mention decimating Phyrne's grass with frost. Who else would have done something so targeted? It may not have been 'magic' so to speak, but the wicked spinster was cheating!

Now here he was, at the witching hour of the morning, preparing a ludicrous and dangerous concoction in the hope that maybe, just maybe, she wouldn't notice he was trying to trick her with a little magic in her drink. Not to get her to stop being her lovely and spiteful self. But maybe… not hate him so damned much.

If he could convince her to drink his famous cider, bespelled to make the drinker fall in love. Well, not love. Not really. A true love potion, those were a thing of myth and legend. But his elixir certainly infatuated the drinker with the first person they laid eyes on. Just a drop or two… Enough to keep his queen from setting off an eternal winter out of spite because she was affronted by a small minded neighbor.

It could work.

Maybe.

It was foolish. He knew it as he added the drops of wishes and infatuation into his cauldron. Some might call it a soup pot. Pot, kettle, cauldron. It didn't matter. She would make him pay through the nose if she ever caught him. He already owed her eternity, flying those stubborn cloven toed cows through the sky every Yule and bringing gifts by the millions across the globe.

But, if he was being honest… The truth was, he enjoyed bringing joy to children. He didn't even mind the red suit and silly hat she'd made him wear to mock him. He didn't belong to the Red Cap Society and probably never would.

Not if Mary Christmas had anything to say about it. It was bad form for Santa to be a Red Cap. Not that most modern humans even knew the significance.

He sighed, spooning ladles full of cider into ceramic mugs. Maybe he should just dump the whole vat down the drain. It wasn't really worth it, was it? This was a delicate magic and could easily go wrong, especially if he was caught.

The buzzing roar of a chain saw split through the silent night like a battle cry. Robin swore as he dropped the mugs, shards of ceramic splintering across his shiny kitchen floor. Apple cinnamon pooled in a spreading brown sheen across the white marble. He grumbled, snatching hand towels out of the drawer and tossing them angrily over the spill. Mopping up the liquid in a rush, he tossed the sodden terry cloths into the laundry sink.

He returned to the stove, still simmering like his own frustration. A second sound joined the whine of the saw blades as it cut into something solid. Not wood, but something more biting, brittle, and *cold*.

Ice.

That stubborn, lying, good for nothing queen, he raged. She really was cheating.

He'd changed his mind. Dangerous or not, he was about to level the playing field. He growled and aggressively ladled a double dose of magic cider into a new mug.

❄ ❄ ❄

The rule was no magic, so Mary would use no magic.

To *decorate* that is.

Robin had neglected to clarify if she could use it to *create* the decoration itself. Just that she wasn't allowed to use it to make anything float, fly, hover, or sparkle with magic. Ice sculptures were a decidedly grey area she intended to exploit.

She had made the globe of ice last night and let it set until just before dawn. Ice, particularly non-magical ice, took a little time to cure. Particularly if you planned to reshape it into something new *without* magic. And she had plans for something new.

Mary flipped the switch on her chainsaw.

The motor roared to life, the feline rumble sending birds fleeing from their trees. Crows cawed in warning up and down the street. Mary's eyes glittered with mischief behind her safety goggles as she set the metal teeth biting into the first chunk of ice.

She delighted in the gentle fall of frozen shards as she carved her first creation. It was not yet time for snow, not in this region, Some years the only snow that came to the

Skagit Valley was because Mary had whispered to the winds, desperate for a taste of home. Hence the magic ice.

"Mary Christmas! What do you think you are you doing?" Phyrne barked.

She was wrapped in a matted grey robe that had seen better years. If Mary had to guess, she'd say it was Phyrne's husband's robe. At least, Mary hoped it was her husband's. Phyrne was a wild card and Mary never could quite predict which way the wind would blow.

For example, this morning the woman was bleary eyed with smudged eyeliner and cracked lipstick. A beige colored eye mask kept the wild nest of bleached blonde tangles at bay beyond her forehead with its over stretched elastic strap. Phyrne pulled the terry cloth robe tighter.

"Decorating," Mary said simply. "Isn't that what you asked me to do?"

"I did not mean for you to get to it at this unholy minute! Some of us need our beauty sleep!" Phyrne had lost all pretense of neighborly politeness.

"Well, be more specific next time," Mary replied as she throttled the motor of her chainsaw until it screamed. She sliced chunks of ice off her slab with gleeful reckless abandon. So what if it ruined the overall effect. She could start over once the viper slithered back to her pond. For now, it was time to play.

Phyrne stomped her foot. "Mary, this is not civilized!"

"I didn't hear any complaints when Robin Goodfellow disassembled his hideous ghoul at an unseemly hour in the morning," she countered. "At least I waited for a Monday." The shriek of exasperation that escaped Phyrne sent a shiver of pleasure straight down Mary's spine.

"Morning, ladies," Robin's velvety baritone purred from the gate.

Phyrne sucked in an alarmed breath. Any irritation Mary felt at the sound of Robin's voice evaporated when she realized how horrified Phyrne was at his very presence. Robin had encountered the poor woman sans makeup and bouffant hair. Mary giggled as Phyrne made futile attempt to smooth her ratted tendrils and wipe away last nights sleep.

"I thought you might enjoy a cup of cider if we're getting up to greet the stars." Robin held out two steaming mugs of fresh mulled cider.

"Oh, thank you," Phyrne simpered, as she accepted the cider. She batted her lashes and turned towards Mary as she blew on the surface of the hot liquid. She must have momentarily forgotten herself because she gave Mary a sincere smile as she sipped from her cup. A devilish smile spread over her cracked lips, and she nodded at Mary.

"I let it simmer all night. Made it just for you," Robin

said. He tucked his hands in his jean pockets, his eyes twinkling in the twilight. Phyrne drank deeper and practically melted in satisfaction.

Mary grabbed the bottom of the mug, not reacting at all to the heat produced by the ceramic as she brought it to her nose and inhaled deeply. It had hints of cloves and orange, cardamon and ginger. The apple-cinnamon floating just beneath the richer spices was positively sinful.

Mary wanted the cider, but she trusted Robin about as far as she could throw him. "What's in it?"

"Cinnamon, ginger, cloves. The usual to ward off evil." Robin grinned.

Mary snorted and sniffed again.

"Nothing of a..." she glanced at Phyrne, who swayed her hips as she enjoyed her beverage and winked at Robin. Mary cringed. "Nothing of a medicinal measure?"

"Would I do that to you?"

"That's not an answer," Mary quipped.

Robin waited patiently and didn't say anything further. He had promised no magic. It was, after all, *his* idea in the first place. She could go out on a little faith. He had always made the most delectable ciders. She blew on the steaming cup once more and sipped.

"This is..." She closed her eyes and wondered at the miracle of the taste. It was a bold heat, perfectly balanced between sweet and tangy. It was like drinking a gingerbread cookie, but better. Mary closed her eyes in appreciation and drank deeper.

"You like it?" Robin cooed, his voice a low rumble in his chest, the heat of his breath brushing by her ear. Mary fluttered her eyes open. Phyrne circled around the blocks of ice, trailing one polished finger over the ribs of frozen water. Her sultry gaze raked over the ice hungrily. Mary smiled.

For the life of her, Mary couldn't recall why she had been so angry with the woman. It was just decorations. She could accommodate Mrs. Nesbitt. It was neighborly after all. And wasn't that why she was here in suburbia? To be a good neighbor.

"Damn it," Robin hissed.

Mary whipped her attention back to the brutish old elf. He scowled at her and at Phyrne. He was ruining a perfectly good morning. The first she'd had with her friendly neighborhood watch captain in ages. The woman was admiring Mary's work. Maybe they could be friends after all. Mary should bake her cookies.

Everyone loved Mary's cookies.

But first, she'd deal with Robin.

"What has your candy cane in a knot?" she demanded.

"Oh, nothing," he groused, scuffing his boot on the soft

grass. "I'm glad you like the cider. You can bring the mugs back when you're finished."

She'd likely throw the tankard through his plate glass windows first. Or maybe she would keep the damn thing as the spoils of war. Mary considered ditching the last dregs of cider by throwing them at his back, but that wasn't very sportsmanly.

And it was unspeakably delicious cider.

"Walk you back, Phyrne?" Robin offered. The woman finally pulled her attention away from the blocks of ice and back to her neighbors. Her face was flushed with cold, her ruddy nose starting to run. She sniffed and wiped it with her sleeve absently, as if she wasn't quite aware of her state of being.

"I'll take her," Mary interjected. She wouldn't have the woman dying of exposure on her watch. They'd miss all the fun of tormenting one another. She shot Robin a puzzled if irritated look and hooked her arm through Phyrne's elbow, guiding them both out the gate and across the road.

The fuzzy feeling wormed its way around her brain and would not quit. She was worried something might be wrong with Phyrne as well as she escorted the woman all the way back to her door. Not that it was a far walk. But Mary just knew something was off. Heavens, what was

Phyrne doing out at this hour? She'd catch her death of cold!

Mary blamed Robin.

"You didn't have to walk me back," Phyrne puffed, a rueful glance over her shoulder. "Mr. Goodfellow would have been just fine." She haughtily tugged at her robe. It had to be her husband's robe. She was wholly unprepared to be outside where other people might see her. And Phyrne was *always* prepared if people might see her.

Mary shook her head. She didn't understand women like Phyrne. Sure, she liked her well enough. As well as one could like a deceitful little toad. But why fawn after idiots like Robin? There were so many more interesting things in the world to be obsessed about and fuss over.

Like tacos. And old fashioned rivalries with your neighbors. Mary quite enjoyed their little feud. It made her feel alive.

"Of course I did," Mary tsked. "We're fast friends."

"We are not friends, Mary," Phyrne hissed back. "You are just the woman who refuses to comply with any of the rules."

"Pish, posh," Mary waved a dismissive hand. "You and I both know rules are for other people. Look at your yard."

"What about my yard?"

"You mean to tell me a million exposed electrical cables

isn't a fire hazard?"

Phyrne's mouth dropped open, a strangled squeak of protest trapped in her throat. Mary grinned wickedly.

"I'm quite certain if we did indeed participate in a *real* HOA, not just our little neighborhood watch squabbles, there would be rules about the magnitude of kilowatts a home could consume on any given Tuesday. So lets not have the kettle call the pot names shall we?" Mary patted Phyrne on the arm. "Cheers, my dear girl. I do so enjoy our little game."

The woman's face turned an ugly shade of red as she struggled to find her voice. Mary left Phyrne gaping and flustered on the front porch. A good days work, in her book. And maybe, just maybe, she could let her petty feud with the neighbor go.

CHAPTER NINE

Three Sisters

No magic was starting to cause problems Mary had not anticipated.

Her ice project lay abandoned after her morning neighborly encounter. Having forgotten all about the ice, she left Phyrne to her own devices and went to make some tea and dress for work.

Her gardening coveralls and a light sweater would at least give the impression she was trying to stay warm. But when she stepped outside all that was left of her globe of ice was a soggy puddle in the grass. There was no way to salvage it. It hadn't occurred to her how warm an autumn morning might be and that non-magic cured ice would melt.

Mary decided ice would have to wait until it was cold enough for the frozen forms to hold their shapes. She pivoted back to her cauldron bubbles as the sun crested above the trees. The delicate glass shimmered in a refracted rainbow of colors and was, pleasantly enough, exactly where she had left it.

Unfortunately, so were the witches. They were currently in a prone state, draped across the lawn, a sad wilted heap of chiffon. Their spindly brooms could be transfigured into giant candy canes with the right ribbons and some tricky bending of their straw bristles. But Mary was reluctant to disassemble the witches entirely because she didn't yet have any inspiration for what to do with them.

Perhaps she'd keep them exactly as they were. Wouldn't it just boil Phyrne's cat if Mary kept the witches up through Christmas? *La Befana* was the perfect Christmas Witch, as anyone from Italy would be the first to tell you. Never mind that Mary was personally responsible for that legend.

"How best to incorporate you ladies into my dreams?" Mary lifted one of her wilted witches into the air, stretching out the delicate fabrics across her chest. She swished tule in the wind like a little girl about to try on her mother's favorite dress, twirling and spinning in a carefree dance.

"I like your witches." It was Cyrus Crabtree from down the street, out for his afternoon walk. He was an Elder member of the Salish Nation and had lived in the corner house for the last forty years. For the crisp autumn afternoon, he wore bright blue jeans and a stiffly collared black shirt. Orange needlepoint threads stitched down his sleeves in the story of his tribe.

"I like them too," Mary agreed, turning from her work to give him her full attention.

"The postman and I saw you were taking the witches down and it brought us sorrow," Cyrus said. He wore his long hair in twin black and silver braids that snaked over his stooped shoulders. They reached nearly to his waist before he tied them with a slip of leather. His brown skin was folded and creased from a life filled with laughter. He brought joy with him wherever he roamed.

"Omar said as much," Mary sighed. "Sadly, I think these ladies need a new life for our next holiday, don't you?"

He weighed her words, his warm honey brown eyes thoughtful. Cyrus had always been considerate like that. Mindful of the impact his words and actions could have. He looked to the sky as if perhaps the answer to her question might be written in the nimbus of the clouds.

"Perhaps you can tell the story of the Three Sisters with your... particular gifts." His smile was knowing and his eyes glimmered with amusement as he returned his bright gaze to Mary. She was quite certain he knew her true name and that she was different. He was respectful of her dual nature though, and he kept it to himself. He chuckled as she draped the gossamer fabric along her fence line, smoothing out the lengths with her fingers.

"The Three Sisters?" Mary asked. His emphasis on each word had made it clear there was a history to these sisters. A lesson in their name. She had lived a long time but had not heard the tale of Three Sisters before. She waited patiently, giving him all the space he might need to find his voice.

"She has many names from many nations, but I have always known her as the Sky Mother. She had three beautiful daughters. Sky Mother's daughters gave us the food of life." Cyrus leaned against Mary's gate. She waited for him to speak again rather than interrupt with questions. He nodded approval and continued.

"The tallest sister gave us corn to stand watch over us." He stretched his arms high above his head to demonstrate.

"The fiercest sister gave us squash to protect us with her sharp edged blades and covered us with her thick arms." He dropped his arms, his strong hands wrapping around the wrought iron posts. He tugged firmly, allowing his arms to support his own body weight as he rocked back on his heels.

"The third sister was whimsical and loved to dance. She gave us beans to twirl around her sisters as she reached her arms to the sun."

"I like these sisters." Mary studied her gauzy figures imagining what they might become. "I think they would make a great addition to my garden."

"I would like to see that," Cyus said. "It would be good for the community to see, don't you agree?"

"Oh certainly," Mary said. It was not lost on her that Thanksgiving might be a troublesome tradition for Mr. Crabtree. That a holiday of celebration for some was also a day of mourning for many. She wasn't sure Cyrus had anyone left to celebrate or mourn with. He rarely had visitors.

"Do you have any plans for Thanksgiving, Mr. Crabtree?" Mary asked.

"I have many plans," Cyrus replied with a wry grin.

"I mean specifically for dinner. I don't often cook a large meal, with only myself to care for. But, if you don't have anywhere to go and I don't have anyone to cook for, we could share a meal instead. A Friends Giving, if you will. I believe that's what the young ones call it."

His hands squeezed tightly around her fence posts and he nodded firmly, tilting his head as though listening to something far away. "I'd like that very much. I'll bring my famous biscuits. You have never had a biscuit as tasty as mine."

"Oh, what a treat that will be!" Mary exclaimed. She loved a good flaky biscuit and was certain they would be the highlight of the meal.

"Good day, Mary Christmas."

"Good day, Mr. Crabtree," Mary said. Cyrus took his leave, shuffling down the street at a leisurely pace.

Mary grinned and immediately set to work. Reshaping the fabric would take some craft and skill. She had a vision for her Three Sisters, now. Each would be bedecked in the leaves of their sacred plant dancing through her garden. Mary would need time and privacy to craft the sculpture in her mind.

She stopped dead in her tracks. She wasn't *supposed* to use magic. But this wasn't really magic. Was it? No, of course not. Not if she did everything by hand. Not if it was out of sight and out of mind. No one wanted to see how sausage was made. Magic could be a similarly ugly process.

Satisfied Robin couldn't accuse her of cheating, Mary took the chiffon and silk inside to dye it. Her gargantuan porcelain sink made an excellent bath to stain each dress. She settled on a gradient of earthy green twining into a deep red before rising into a buttery dawn of honey-gold. The red hem melting into the gold gave the impression of a gilded fire. She hung the gowns near the oven to dry.

While the dresses were drying, she began braiding the hair. On her recent visit to the craft store, Mary had grabbed a roll of mesh wire made of moldable plastics along with a stockpile of corn husks and green fronds... Just in case. She'd had no practical purpose for them at the time. It seemed serendipity and intuition had guided her impulse buy.

She bent the mesh into three crowns, each with a slightly different variations. The corn husks and river fronds wove intimately into braids she fastened to the crowns with glittering amber, emerald, and ruby jewels. Real ones, so they would wink and twinkle even in starlight.

After each sister was properly crowned, she fastened a necklace of leaves around their shoulders. Blades of green from corn husks for the oldest. Sharply edged leaves the size of a man's palm for the middle sister, and delicate teardrop petals for the youngest.

Mary stepped outside, pleased as punch. She was positively *giddy* about her Three Sisters. Cyrus had given her just the right mundane magic to refresh her witches into something fantastical. If Phyrne was going to have a perfectly beige Christmas, Mary would do the opposite.

All the colors. All the shapes. A Yuletide extravaganza.

Take *that* city ordinances.

The brooms were exactly where she had left them, stiffly stacked beside the cauldron. With a few strategically arranged branches Mary was able to get her Three Sisters upright again. She took her time, arranging the Sisters so they could dance and drift around the cauldron. With their freshly dyed gowns and crowns of fronds, they balanced whimsy and tradition effortlessly. Mary finished securing their gradient chiffon and green frond ribbons as the last rays of daylight winked out behind the trees.

At that exact moment, Phyrne puffed around the corner at a jog. She wore a *Fabletics* jumpsuit of bright orange, pink, and yellow. Mary had to blink several times just to recover from the colorful ocular onslaught. Phyrne slowed to a glacial pace, half jogging in place. Her eyes glazed over in a feral glint as she stared at Mary's latest additions.

"Evening, Mrs. Nesbitt," Mary called out cheerfully.

"What. Is. That?" Phyrne hissed.

"Like it? I thought we needed something to tie Thanksgiving to Christmas. They're called *The Three Sisters*," Mary calmly outlined. "They were Mr. Crabtree's idea." She smiled broadly at Phyrne, daring her to say anything.

Phyrne stopped running. Her chest rose and fell with

each shallow breath as she tugged at her synthetic neon top, stretching the material back where it belonged. She looked down the street to the corner house.

Mr. Crabtree was quietly gardening in the fading sunlight. As if he could sense the women's gazes, he lifted his head and looked in their direction. His expression was neutral, but the cheerful salute he sent their way was enough. Phyrne knew. Mary knew. She had won. Again.

"You need lights," Phyrne commented before continuing with her jog.

"I'm sorry?" Mary asked confused.

Phyrne paused in the middle of the road, treading in place and tossing her hair carelessly. "You haven't hung any lights. You need Christmas lights. Otherwise, it's just junk. I'm sure Robin can help you if you're too worried about falling and breaking a hip to climb a ladder."

Mary's jaw fell open as Phyrne made her way across the street. It was a good thing her mortal shock won out over pure rage, otherwise Phyrne would have made a blazing neon addition to Mary's garden gnome collection.

The rules of magic be damned.

CHAPTER TEN

All the Trimmings

An hour later, Mary was delighted to discover the local hardware store had plenty of lights. A wide array of displays which nearly overwhelmed her senses the very moment she walked through their sliding glass doors. Surrounded by an incandescent blaze of luminations, she had spent twenty minutes spinning in a circle trying to make a decision before a helpful gentleman on staff took pity on her.

"Yeah, these ones here," he thumbed a meaty fist at a shelf full of boxes. "You can link your smart phone right up. Make them colors dance to whatever tune you fancy." He had a bulbous nose and a portly belly. The name tag on his cherry red vest said Chuck.

"Of course you may need your grandkids to help hook it up. I myself was boondoggled for over an hour before I called mine," the man drawled.

"These may be overkill, don't you agree?" Mary was not about to ask any neighbors, children or otherwise, for help with the damned lights.

"Nah, it's only one strand. Long enough to cover the whole front of your house. There will even be a few lengths left to connect to an outlet. You don't need more than one," Chuck insisted. "Not like some of them folks who nab up all the boxes on the shelf and blow the power grid for the night." He laughed.

"Yes, quite unneighborly," Mary agreed.

She would absolutely be taking the entire shelf.

"You wanna see what they can do?"

"Why not?" Mary gave him an inhuman smile of feral beauty that made his skin flush pink.

Chuck led her to an area where a variety of Christmas ornaments and lawn decorations were displayed on the floor. Dozens more were suspended above their heads with cables. A ten-by-ten village of trees and miniature houses were decked as thoroughly as any kindergarten gingerbread experiment. Mary tilted her head thoughtfully as Chuck waddled over to a stand wrapped in lights with an official "STAFF ONLY" sign in bold block letters.

He grabbed a brick of a remote and pushed several buttons, gesturing for Mary to stand back to observe the full effect. She raised an eyebrow, pursing her lacquered lips in amusement as she indulged him. Chuck cranked a dial and Mary jumped as her senses were accosted.

"Whoa-oh-oh-oh!" *WHOMP*. The music and lyrics from "The Greatest Showman" began an intricate ballet of sound and light. Every thump of the beat, every trebled lyric changed the color of the lights. The spiral of trees, all crafted out of rope lights and wire branches. Twinkling lights plunged up and down and around, each branch blinking in time to the music in a hypnotic concussion of color.

"See how it pulses with the music?" Chuck gestured at the display with his fist. "This here is more of an orchestrated performance than your everyday light 'em up decorations." He was shouting to be heard, louder than the pounding of the music. Mary had to resist the urge to cover her ears.

"It is quite stimulating," Mary fired back. She was going to need a spot of tea with a dash of something stronger just to bring her own system back online.

"It sure is," Chuck agreed with a grin. He turned down the dial and the volume returned to a manageable decibel.

"And this is all intended for outdoors? The exterior of a

home?" Mary asked.

"Yep."

"So, I just put them up... And they play music?"

"Well that's where your grandkids come in," Chuck puffed. "You'll need one of them smart phones, and a blue-tooth speaker or some such thing. The kids will set it in a pattern. Just let 'em do their thing with the digital doo-hickeys. *Magic!*" Chuck popped his hands in the air, spreading his fingers in a fan to emphasize the word *magic*.

"Magic, indeed," Mary agreed.

In the end, Mary bought fifteen of the boxes even though Chuck protested, insisting she only needed one. He obviously had never been to her neighborhood at Christmas. But he patiently helped her load her vintage blue Jag trunk to near bursting with the boxes and wished her luck.

With the competition on her mind, Mary descended on the farmers market next to see what interesting bits and baubles she might find. It was still early in the season but there was always at least one vendor who couldn't wait to hawk their holiday wares. Some people started selling Christmas in July.

It didn't take Mary long to find exactly the right thing. Sculpted eight pointed Bethlehem stars as big as a small child were crafted from silver wires and cubic zirconia.

She'd bought the craftswoman out of her stock and ordered more to be delivered to her home as soon as possible. She had managed to stuff two into her car's side passenger seat, and the third in her tiny bench seat behind the driver. It was a tight fit, but it was a short trip up the hill to home.

She hadn't made it five minutes down the shady avenue when Mary Christmas had to hit the brakes. The sudden jolt was hard enough the back end of her Jaguar slipped and left rubber tread marks on the blacktop. She only regretted her choice in decorations a teensy tiny bit as the sharp point of a star pricked the back of her neck.

There in the middle of the road, a gang of wild turkeys meandered at a lazy pace. They strut and garbled, indifferent to traffic. Mary and the Subaru Forrester facing the opposite direction had halted suddenly and completely, with no shoulder or passing lane.

Impatient drivers behind both vehicles blared their horns. Everyone knew it was most likely turkeys, as opposed to a magically appearing invisible stop sign. It didn't stop them from laying on their horns in a futile attempt to convince the birds to move. Mary glared in her rearview mirror until the construction truck behind her stopped.

The turkeys were undeterred by the bellowing vehicles

or the complaints of their passengers. They weren't even bothered by the imminent threat of steal and squashed turkey as Mary inched her vehicle forward. One bird had the audacity to peck its ruddy beak at her grill plate.

Yes, the turkeys ruled this land.

Turkeys were not native birds to the Pacific Northwest. They'd been brought over on wagons and migrated with colonizers as they spread out across the continent. The birds found they liked it here and turned river valleys into their own special mating ground. Despite the growing human population and the ever encroaching buildings, the birds would not be moved. They had continued to increase and multiply their flocks no matter what Fish and Wildlife did. The birds ruled the roads.

Then, Mary had an absolutely marvelous idea.

Maybe she could talk to them. Wildspeak, a gift that allowed certain magical folk to communicate with animals, had never been one of her particular gifts, as far she knew. Although the reindeer always seemed to listen and understand her. How else did you get them to fly? Cats also seemed inclined to linger and listen. Or, perhaps the neighbors Devon Rex just really enjoyed patrolling her old Victorian craftsman for mice. Mary parked her vintage Jaguar, unbuckling and stepping out to have a little chat with the flock of poultry.

"I have a proposition for you." The turkeys turned their heads towards her. Well, she had their attention at least. "I have it on good authority you enjoy a nice deciduous tree. Occasionally, some holly berries, yes?"

The flock shuddered as if in response. She wasn't sure if they spoke English or pheromones. Frankly, she wasn't even sure they could understand her. But they were responding. Perhaps she did have the gift of wildspeak after all.

The Subaru driver had started filming her on their cellphone. Mary knew she would look like a crazy old lady yelling at a flock of turkeys. What did she care? Mary had plans for her feathered friends. She waved at the Subaru driver and continued speaking to the birds.

"If you would kindly move yourselves off the road and find your way to Washington Street, there is a little beige house three doors in. You can't miss it. There is an abundance of boxwood bushes and holly berries a plenty. I know it would just make the perfect roost for your magnificent family."

The turkeys warbled and called to one another, scuttling across the asphalt and into the bushes. They disappeared as Mary closed the door to her jaguar, grinning like a Cheshire Cat.

The joy lasted all the way home.

CHAPTER ELEVEN

Sugar and Spice

It had been over a week since she had purchased her Christmas lights and then promptly began to ignore them. She hadn't gotten far in her work with Christmas. Not using her magic had left her feeling drained, her muscles stiff and aching after she spent time working.

How did normal people function? It wasn't civilized.

She flitted from project to project, unable to get anything done because it all took so much more time without her magic. She'd get half a task done and then be forced to recover with tea and a book while her body mended itself.

By Sunday Mary was exhausted and uninspired. She knew she needed to let off some steam and use her gifts or they would consume her. So, it was time to bake cookies.

She marched into her kitchen and became a whirlwind of activity.

"Where is the sugar!" Mary boomed.

She had every cupboard in her exquisite kitchen thrown wide open. It was a warm earthy space with butter cream walls accented by hand painted tiles. Each tile was decorated with garden herbs in vibrant colors. Their scientific names were written in a golden flowery script.

Dark wood floors and white washed floating cabinets were paired against black appliances. Fresh herbs from Mary's garden hung twined in bundles from dark wood beams. It looked like a witch's cottage. Mary supposed it was, in some regards.

Even so, she could never find *anything*.

She huffed a breath of frustration and continued opening cupboards. The plan today had been to make her famous shortbread cookies. No baker in the world could compare to Mary for her shortbread. The bakers in France came close with their decadent Madelines. The delightful Ma'amoul made in the Arab world were even closer, their nut and honeyed treasures folded inside a powdery dough. But no one came close to the magic of Mary Christmas's shortbread cookies.

If she could just find her damned ingredients.

It was a rather simple cookie. Flour, sugar, loads of

buttery goodness. A touch of nutmeg and cinnamon. And, when she was feeling particularly festive, a dash of magic. Maybe a hit of powdered sugar if she was feeling whimsical at the end.

Her lips curled in wicked delight. Anyone who ate one of her cookies was at her mercy. Of course she only gave them to very special individuals who needed her help. It would be an outrageous crime to give them to just *anyone*. But for those who needed to redefine love, unpack their past, or discover their own power it was a gift.

She made her magic cookies exclusively for those who needed them most.

"Where is the damned sugar!"

There was a knock on her door, light and tentative. As if the uninvited guest knew she was in a mood. Or maybe they just heard her shouting. Mary dusted her hands on her apron and headed for the kitchen door.

Standing beyond her threshold, Robin looked fresh and unbothered. She stared at him, temper choking off her thoughts.

Robin took a step back, weariness in his eyes as he ran a nervous hand through effortlessly tousled brown hair. He grinned, highlighting the stubble on his jaw. He wore blue jeans and a cozy red and black plaid shirt unbuttoned to his sternum. He looked like a lumber snack.

"What do you want?" Mary snapped, irritated at the very sight of his handsome face.

Robin lifted a heavy brown paper sack into view. "Groceries," he offered.

"I don't need groceries," Mary groused. "I need—"

Robin reached into the depths of his bag and pulled out a two pound bag of granulated raw sugar. Mary gaped and Robin's lips twitched in merriment.

"May I come in?" he asked sweetly.

Mary didn't answer, just turned on her heel and stalked back into the heart of her home. She heard the door latch behind her and the stomp of his heavy boots as he cleared the debris on her mat before following her inside.

She didn't have any space to unpack his bag. The quartz counters were covered in various baking supplies. None of which she needed. An over sized bag of baking soda she had been portioning into smaller more manageable containers had tipped over next to the mixing bowls. Three different bowls were stacked in ascending order, their glass hollows empty and waiting. Every spice in the pantry had been unearthed, but not one of them was the nutmeg she required.

On the stove was a pot set to simmer with the half used carton of buttermilk. She had been in the middle of making her own butter when she remembered she wasn't sure where the sugar was. And in her distracted half finished projects, the pot had boiled off all the milk. The pot was burned, and the butter ruined.

Mary stomped over to the stove and turned off the burner. Today, she just couldn't get anything right. It was very unlike her. Mary was ready to take out her irritation on the nearest target. She rounded on Robin in a frustrated glower.

"I see it's cookie day," he said mildly as he unearthed ingredients from his paper sack.

"Obviously," she lamented, leaning against the stove. She swept a loose white curl out of her eyes with the back of her hand. It had stubbornly insisted on escaping its pins, and Mary had given up on getting it to stay.

"I was hoping to come to a truce," Robin began. He had somehow acquired everything she needed. He set the bag of raw sugar crystals beside her baking bowls and unearthed a wax paper wrapping of a yellow brick.

"What's this?" Mary asked, as he offered it to her. She took the package and sniffed. "Is it really?"

"Butter. Freshly packed from County Cork in Ireland"

"How in the stars did you get Kerrygold butter, fresh, at this hour of the morning?" Mary wanted to know.

"I do have a flying sleigh and eight reindeer," Robin said with a grin. Mary blew a raspberry at him. Robin noticed there was nowhere to really set any of the ingredients he had procured for her. "How do you find anything in this mess?"

"It's my process," Mary said defensively. She dropped the butter on the counter beside the stove and set about organizing her workspace. Robin moved to help. She smacked his hand. "Stop. You'll mess it up."

"As opposed to how it is now?" Robin said, sliding a box of cookie cutters out of the way.

"If you break anything…" Mary warned.

"I know, I know." Robin continued unpacking the flour, the sugar, the Ceylon cinnamon dust wrapped up in a silk pouch.

In a moment that lasted an eternity, Mary watched in horror as her brain refused to register what she was seeing. She could stop it. She could save it, if only she could just *move*. Robin shoved aside the bowl of melting ice she had set out for the butter making. The jostled bowl of ice knocked the empty canister she used for storing sugar. The canister bumped into the pile of cutting boards, which tumbled like dominos. The force of it sent her favorite moonstone crystal rolling pin spinning. It thumped onto the counter with an echoing boom as it rolled to the edge and plummeted to the tile floor with a thunderous *crack*. The rolling pin fractured into a dozen pieces.

"What did you do?" Mary cried in breathless horror.

Mary fell to her knees and scooped the slivered pieces close to her heart. It had been her mother's rolling pin, a family heirloom passed down to Mary lifetimes ago. She had used it for years, lovingly polishing the stone to a shine after each use. Proudly rolling out magical cookies every year. Mary had always suspected that the cookies she made were largely of a higher quality *because* of her mother's moonstone rolling pin.

Her horror and despair turned to rage, her blood running cold as her face burned hotter and hotter. She clutched the crystal halves to her chest.

"Get. Out."

"What?" Robin asked, oblivious to the damage he had done.

"This is my mother's rolling pin. It is the last of its kind and the only thing I have left of her," Mary said, a rumble of pressure building in her chest. In answer, thunder clapped outside and rattled the windows. "And you, in your carelessness broke it."

His face drained of color as Robin realized the severity of his mistake. "I didn't mean to—"

"Get. Out!" Mary screamed. A blast of icy wind threw wisps of flour into a frenzy. Anything not anchored crashed off the counters in a rain of splintering glass.

Robin didn't hesitate to obey. He left whatever else might be in the bag of groceries unattended and fled the kitchen.

A sticky wet substance trickled down her face. Mary couldn't bring herself to care. She was shattered. As shattered as her kitchen. As broken as the pieces of her mother's rolling pin. The last shard of her old life obliterated.

She swept her gaze over the ruined heart of her home. Shards of glass from broken bowls lay scattered across the tile. Mounds of flour swept into sloping dunes like sand. Grains of sugar and nutmeg blanketed the counters and floors.

Mary found her feet, struggling to make herself even exert the energy to stand. She picked her way across the ruined mess, trailing a mist of milled flour and sugar as she went. She set the broken pieces of her heart on the hall table as she trudged up the stairs.

The rolling pin was ancient, so old Mary could hardly remember a time in her life when it wasn't there. It was the last shred of her mother, her former self. And it was gone. She wished desperately she could repair it, but it was impossible. A solid slab of moonstone could not be unbroken.

She couldn't fix this. She couldn't bake. Couldn't even

find it in her heart to torment the neighbors with the extreme length of lights and oversized stars she had bought. She needed… something else.

She'd start by getting herself cleaned up. The large clawfoot bath was made for someone twice her size. She turned the faucet to scalding and let it run. Her clothes she threw in the trash. It wasn't worth the effort of picking out the bits of glass she may or may not be able to find.

While steam began to curl through the air gently but efficiently warming the ensuite, Mary stepped in front of the full length mirror. Her face was streaked with tears and flour. A shard of glass had pierced her cheek and a bead of blood trickled from the wound. She plucked out the glass and tossed it in the rubbish bin beside the sink.

When the tub was full, she added drops of oil scented with lavender and tea tree to sooth the hurt. Then a scoop of Epsom salt to soothe the ache. It stung in a dozen different places as she stepped into the steaming liquid. She welcomed the pain, to feel anything but the dead emptiness that opened like a chasm inside her. It was her temper that had done the damage to her skin, but the damage to her soul, she wasn't sure what might heal that.

She knew, somewhere in her heart of hearts, Robin had not been *trying* to make things worse. He had been *trying* to make it better. But he *had* made it so much worse. He had stolen the last piece of her humanity. The last piece of her that belonged to the woman she used to be before becoming something new, something cold. She wasn't sure she could ever forgive him for it.

Heat soaked into her bones until she was pink and flushed from head to toe. The scented lavender and tea tree drops drifted through the air in a steaming mist that clouded the mirror and windows. It was so hot it bordered on uncomfortable. She didn't care. The pain let her know she was still alive.

Mary slipped beneath the surface, holding her breath as the heat washed over her. Winter was her power but sometimes the flame of heat helped calm her. It soothed and settled the icy core of her powerful and destructive gifts until she could manage them. Use them for good, rather than be consumed by them.

Under normal circumstances, Robin would be the balance of warmth and joy to her unyielding cold. It was how she had come to utilize his special gifts as the Claus. His own unyielding warmth balanced her never ending cold. His gifts allowed her to create magic the world could only experience in the dead of winter.

But today…

She really hoped the bath would give her back some sense of self.

She let a whisper of air escape her, one bubble at a time. The spheres rolled up until they broke the viscus surface with a pop. She opened her mouth and screamed, the air boiling to the surface in an icy torrent. The warmth gone from her bath, Mary shivered and heaved her way out of the water, sopping and dreadful.

She wrapped a towel around her hair and tied off a thick robe of cerulean blue. It made her eyes ignite like beacons of azure ice as she passed by her vanity on the way to her walk in closet.

Motion in the street attracted her attention to the window. Buttery sunlight melted through her sheer curtains and washed the carpeted floor in golds. She secured the belt of her robe and peered out through a sliver of gossamer fabric, careful to stay hidden by the wall.

Robin was in his driveway splitting wood and stacking it in pyramids. How much wood did he need to heat that monster of a house? It was brand new. Mary knew he couldn't possibly need that much wood to heat that home. Not unless he was as completely useless as a carpenter as he was as the Claus today.

She realized that was unfair. He hadn't intended her or her heart harm. He had in fact been trying to make amends with a gift. She sighed as he split another cord of wood with the practiced grace of a Viking king. It took hardly any effort at all. Mary continued watching him work until that meddlesome neighbor Phyrne stopped her beige SUV to chat.

Mary growled and turned aside. She wasn't sure who she was more upset with. Robin, Phyrne, or herself. She shook her head to rid herself of those pesky feelings. She needed to start with herself if she was going to get through this day without murder.

Mary went back into her bedroom, sliding open the pocket door to her closet and examining her options. What did one wear to clean up the mess she'd made from an immortal temper tantrum? Jeans, sweater, boots. That would have to do.

She selected a thick cable of Granny apple green Aran knit sweater and a pair of jeans that had started to fray at the ankles. She didn't wear blue jeans often, but these were old enough that it didn't matter what she got on them.

Someone had told her once that they were vintage Levi's and she could sell them for a pretty penny. She had just smiled politely. You can't exactly admit the jeans you wear casually when the mood suits you were the first sample from the original manufacturer. They had been made specifically as a gift. Levi only existed because Mary helped him launch the brand.

She stepped into comfy socks and stuffed her feet into

heavy boots and shuffled toward the kitchen. In her reluctance to get started, she kept her eyes firmly on the carpet. When her feet hit the tile she froze.

Some part of her had blocked out the disaster that was her kitchen where she made her famous cookies. Only the cherished few were allowed to visit her hearth. Where she showed the people she loved how she felt by offering them a homemade meal.

The very heart of her home was destroyed.

Mary needed to get out.

CHAPTER TWELVE

Mrs. Claus

Mary needed to cool her raging thoughts. She could just continue outside, finish her decorating project. There was plenty of fresh air, but the work was just different. You sweat. You toil. And the scenery only changed when you nailed it to the post.

She needed something truly different.

A brisk walk was in order. She made it six houses before a shrieking cry of protest ricocheted through the air. The cozy cottage across the street was starting to show its age around the edges. The yard was littered with children's summer toys that had not quite made it into storage yet, the family stubbornly holding out until the first frost.

Or maybe they were just too tired from parenting to care.

The front screen door slammed against the exterior wall as two boys went barreling into the house, bikes discarded on the lawn. They loudly complained the other had pushed them or hit them. The story changed as they talked over one another.

Through the open door, Mary could see their mother Selena kneeling in front of her six-year-old, Magdelena. The littlest Ortiz was loudly wailing on the floor at her mother's feet. Her two older brothers, Jax and Carlos, were shouting over her tears about who was at fault.

"She got in the way again! She always gets in the way!" Jax shouted.

Selena pursed her full lips together as she fussed over her youngest's injury, glancing up at her boys. The look in her eyes warned them she was in no mood for their stories. The boys paid her no mind as they continued to profess their innocence.

Selena had her silky brown hair hastily tied up in a messy bun. She wore purple sweats with a gold W stamped on the thigh from University of Washington. The fabric bunched loosely around her hips and knees. Her feet were in well worn grey Ugg boots that were starting to fray at the seams. Her lavender razor back tank hugged her soft curves. Her honey brown eyes were tired, a dark patch of weariness muting their warmth.

Harried and exhausted were the words that popped to mind as Mary watched her work. She had seen Selena towing little Magdelena in a wagon and chasing after the older ones on their bikes. The boys were often racing to the park at the end of the block abandoning their sister to trail after them. Hours later, the children were still running circles around their mother. Selena could barely keep up.

In the breath of a moment, Mary forgot all about Robin, her shattered rolling pin and the desecrated kitchen. She could do little to change what happened. She could do even less about the fate of the world. It was the burden and the curse of her magic. Powerful enough to change the shape of matter or shift the temperament of the wind. Powerless to change how the world worked.

But she could fix one mother's day.

Mary marched up the front steps.

"It wasn't our fault!" Carlos insisted.

"It's never your fault!" Magdelena shouted back.

"Enough, *mija*," Selena snapped, her mezzo voice thundering through the room. The children went quiet.

Mary knocked on the open door's frame.

Selena turned an exasperated look toward the door. Her eyes were wild, caught between tears, shock, and manners. Manners won as she realized who was on the threshold. She shushed her children and plastered on a fake smile.

"Mary Christmas. What can I do for you?" she asked.

Mary flicked her gaze over the home. The kitchen was as big a disaster as Mary's. She'd caught Selena in the middle of meal prepping. Bowls of chopped vegetables were left half attended as she cobbled together spare ingredients for the evening meal. The adjacent living room was littered with toys and discarded school books. Half finished homework was stacked haphazardly on the coffee table under a precarious sippy cup of juice.

"It seems I am just in time." Mary shut the door firmly behind her. "I am here to ask how I can help *you*."

Selena's shoulders were slumped forward. The secret burden of every mother was they needed all the help but felt too ashamed to ask. And, even if they did ask, more shameful that they needed help in the first place.

In the blink of an eye, Mary knew where her growing frustration with Robin brewed. The invisible labor of mothers across the globe, especially during the holidays, and the men, the fathers, getting credit for providing the magic of it. Santa gets all the credit. But it is nearly always Mother who makes Christmas sparkle.

It made Mary's blood boil.

"It looks as though you might be able to use an extra hand," Mary offered.

Selena eyed her suspiciously. She supposed it was to be

expected. Mary was the eccentric neighbor who showered the children with candy on Halloween. Mary had petty feuds with the neighbors for no good reason other than it was fun. On the surface, it had to look pretty odd.

"I have an idea," Mary said. "Why doesn't Mama go and put her feet up, or take a hot bath while I finish up dinner here?"

"You know how to make *posole*?" Selena asked, suspicious.

"I'm quite sure I can manage," Mary assured her.

Selena was dubious. Jax agreed, rattling off the reasons why Mary couldn't possibly prepare the hearty soup in rapid fire Spanish.

One of her many talents allowed Mary to understand almost any language without any true effort on her part. Though, to be fair, *who is this crazy white lady* followed by *be quiet* really needed no translation on her part.

Mary gave the children a fiendish grin and clapped her hands to her chest, the perfect picture of a wicked winter Queen. "Children, do you know why they call me Mary Christmas?"

Selena looked from Mary to her children and back. The children's faces were mistrustful but Mary had their attention. There was a certain kind of magic, the disbelief of the modern child. You could be forthright and honest with them, they still would never fully believe you were telling the truth. But Mary could maybe help these little ones believe in magic. Just a touch.

"Why's that?" Jax, the oldest and boldest of the tiny crew stepped forward. He had his mother's eyes and his fathers mouth. It was difficult to say where exactly he got the sharp jaw and hawklike nose, because his parents both had rounder features, but that expression was every bit his mother.

"It's because I am *the* Mary Christmas. Though you may know me by another name."

She had them now. Little Magdelena had stopped crying. Jax and Carlos had crept forward hanging on her every word.

"Sometimes, I am called *Frau Perchta* in Germany, *La Befana* in Italy, *Babushka* in Russia, and Mother Christmas in some secret places you can only dream of. But you, my dearest children, may call me Mrs. Claus."

Their eyes popped in disbelief and wonder.

"Bullshit!" Jax scoffed.

"*Mijo!*" Selena rebuked him.

"If she's Mrs. Claus, what's she doing in this dinky town?" he demanded.

"I believe her!" Magdelena was not about to leave it up to chance that Santa wouldn't visit because her brother ruined it for her. Mary smiled at the fierce girl. If only all children kept that precious innocent faith past the age of five.

"Of course she's Mrs. Claus, *mijo*." Selena, bless her, had realized immediately she was caught between confirming the weird neighbor was in fact a fairy tale creature… or admitting to her six, eight, and ten-year-old Santa wasn't real. "You've clearly never had one of Mary's cookies."

"I've had her cookies!" Magdelena looked hopeful.

"Her cookies, Mama?" Jax asked. He and his brother Carlos were still reluctant, but losing their battle with doubt. Mom was involved now. Selena made a gesture with her fingers, fanning them out and twisting her wrist in the air as if snow were falling.

"Magic," Selena said with a warm smile.

"And, since I am *the* Mrs. Claus, I have a certain amount of sway with a certain gentleman who favors a red coat. We'll call him Santa. He's always very interested in what I have to say about the possible wishes tiny humans like you might desire…" Mary looked each of them in the eye sternly. "So, we are going to finish the chores while Mama goes and takes a hot bath, yes?"

They all nodded vigorously.

"Excellent!" Mary clapped her hands and gestured for Selena to vacate the kitchen. She sent a feathers breath spell of *trust* through the room and Selena relaxed. She patted Magdelena on the head and walked briskly from the room.

"All right, my little heathens, shall we?"

Mary had agreed that she would not use her magic in the decorating of *her* home. She had not agreed to a complete cease fire of her magic *everywhere*. It was an ambiguous grey area if she used magic on a good cause *for* her neighbors. Magic was funny that way. Specifics. It required very detailed specifics. Mary grinned at her twisted cleverness.

The first task was to encourage the children away from the kitchen. Mary had her minions sorting toys into bins, organizing book shelves, and generally scrubbing their main living room in a harmony of cleaning noises while Mary worked in the kitchen. Whenever there was a pause to see if Mary was still listening, she would start singing loudly…

"He's making a list, checking it twice!"

"Gonna find out who's naughty and nice!" Magdelena would finish. The vacuum would promptly turn back on.

An hour later, everything was spot shined and placed exactly where their mother had always wanted it. The children returned to the kitchen to find dinner ready, Thanksgiving meal preparations had been portioned and stored in the refrigerator. And her famous shortbread cookies were rolled, cut, and set on a baking sheet.

"How?" Jax and Carlos asked in absolute awe.

"Mama told you." Magdelena was delighted by the possibilities and bound into the space with enthusiasm. She used the pine wood step stool to get to the counter and claimed a finger full of dough from the ceramic mixing bowl. She sighed pleasantly and turned adoring eyes to Mary.

"Magic," they said together.

Thoroughly satisfied with a job well done, Mary popped the cookies into the oven just as Selena made her way into the kitchen. Her wet hair was wrapped in a towel, her fresh clothes clean and comfortable. She hadn't seen Selena that relaxed in a while. Weeks at the very least. Maybe longer.

Selena didn't say anything, her eyes roaming over the tidy kitchen and adjacent living room. Jax, Carlos, and Magdelena were quietly playing with a giant floor puzzle, speaking in low tones. Selena finally returned to Mary, who smugly dusted her hands free of the last loose bits of flour and unfastened the bakers apron she'd found tucked behind the pantry door.

"The cookies only need twelve minutes exactly. Let them rest on the pan to cool for at least six more. Helps crisp the bottoms," she instructed matter-of-factly. "They'll be good warm or cold. Just don't take them off the pan too soon or they're bound to crumble into bits."

Mary gave Selena a warm smile, handing off her apron to the lady of the house. It felt good to do something kind for someone. Selena still hadn't found her voice. Mary nodded crisply before striding toward the door. She snatched her green coat off the back of the couch where she'd left it.

"Wait," Selena finally said.

She grabbed Mary by the arm as she was turning, the green wool settling over her shoulders with minimal effort. Mary was keenly aware of the young eyes on them. Selena must have sensed it too because she dropped her gaze back to her children, a curious and baffled expression on her face. She looked at Mary with the purest gratitude.

"Thank you... *Señora* Christmas."

"It was my absolute pleasure dear," Mary replied honestly. She turned the large brass door knob, swinging open the door only to be confronted with Mr. Ortiz. He was as startled to see Mary as she was to find him. "Such a pleasant evening, isn't it, Mateo?"

"It is," he managed to say, holding the door for her as she stepped into the rapidly cooling night air.

The door hadn't quite finished closing when Mary heard

them exchange in accelerated Spanish. Mary didn't need her gift to interpret when little Magdelena shouted, "Mrs. Claus made us cookies!"

CHAPTER THIRTEEN

Brownies

Mary felt utterly satisfied by a job well done. It had been some time since she had actively engaged in making life easier for someone deserving of her gifts, like the Ortiz family. Perhaps she could find other ways to do more.

She made it three steps toward home when she remembered what waited for her. A decimated kitchen. Ruined spices and dry goods flung into every crevice. Shattered pieces of her old life.

Her mother's rolling pin.

All the rage came surging back.

She felt frost nip at her fingertips and she shook her hands sending shards of ice raining against the pavement like pebbles. She wasn't ready to face her home. She wasn't ready to clean up what had been left behind. But if not now, then when? Never.

She would never be ready.

The beating echo of a hammer against wood pounded through the neighborhood like a battering ram. Robin was in his driveway again, constructing some sort of structure out of recycled planks of pine. By the look of it, a small ecurie to go with the wooden cut outs of Jesus, Mary, and Joseph he'd made for Phyrne's yard last week.

Mary growled and marched straight for him.

He didn't notice her approach under the rhythmic beat of his hammer against the wood. It took him little time and minimal effort to finalize the frame of the ecurie arches. She watched him work for several swings, waiting for him to acknowledge her. When he didn't, she snapped.

"You and I need to have a chat," Mary said coldly.

Robin lifted his head up to look at her, his sea dark eyes shadowed like a storm. He continued working, hammering nails into wood with an angry swing. "Right now?"

"You don't think so?" Mary asked.

"I do, but not if you're just going to yell at me," Robin said. He wasn't looking at her, his focus entirely on his work.

She wanted to know what exactly he felt gave him the right to be mad at *her* right now.

"Perhaps we should take this inside then, if you don't wish the neighbors to witness your queen, what was the phrase?" Mary paused, as if trying to remember, her head tilted to one side as she narrowed her eyes to dangerous slits. "Ah, yes. 'Yell' at you."

"I thought you didn't want to be called by your title where ears might hear," Robin said, unfazed.

"I'm done being polite," Mary said, her voice as frosty as her veins.

Robins mouth thinned into a line and his blue eyes darkened to the blackest blue of a raging sea. He raised his chin in momentary defiance before closing his eyes and inclining his head in a curt formal nod. "Yes, my queen. Won't you join me inside for a cup of cider?"

Mary considered his invitation for a long lethal moment. They were old creatures, Mary Christmas and Robin Goodfellow. The rules that governed them kept their powers from leaking out into the world. Hospitality and manners must be observed.

Especially by Mary Christmas.

She stalked past him and into his home. Guesting laws or not, she would not wait or bow for him.

It didn't take long for Robin to store his tools and join her. Mary waited, her patience growing thin. She strategically claimed the overly large chair angled just right to rule over the whole house with a mere turn of the head. She settled delicately on the arm of the chair rather than allow the supple brown leather to swallow her in its comforting embrace.

From her perch, she had to make no effort to view his approach through the large plate windows or flick her eyes to the turning knob as he opened the exterior door that lead from his garage to the kitchen. He pushed through the heavy oak door, pausing to stomp his boots on the mat before he crossed the threshold and looked at her.

Every movement grated her temper.

"Why do you insist on working for that toadstool of a woman?" Mary demanded as soon as he the door snicked shut behind him.

Robin, smartly, did not respond immediately. Instead he removed his coat and hung it on the hook beside the door. He then methodically began washing his hands and forearms in the sink gazing out the window.

He had a direct line of sight to Mary's house from that window. She had spied him washing dishes or covertly observing the neighborhood from that exact spot a time or two. But from this angle, she could not read his expression, his mouth and eyes carefully neutral.

"Well? I'm waiting," she reminded him.

Robin dried his hands on a towel before he turned to

face her. He swept a stoic gaze around the open room, taking inventory and delaying his answer.

Mary grated her teeth. She hated waiting. It was her trick and her right to make Robin, or anyone she wished really, wait for *her*. She started counting in her head.

1… 2… 3…

If she got to five she was definitely turning him into a gnome for her garden.

"What does it matter?" Robin finally asked quietly.

"Excuse me?"

"I work for a lot of people in the off season. What does it matter, my queen?"

"Yes, but that woman and I are in a…"

"War?" Robin asked, a mocking tip to the corners of his mouth.

"That's a word for it. Yes. A decorating war. Why in this world would you want to be on team toadstool when you truly work for me?"

"What is it you object to, my queen?"

"You are helping her with her beige and lifeless decor. You're making her useless imagination come alive."

"Am I not the Claus? Is it not my job to bring Christmas to the world?"

There's the rub. Mary found herself in a terrible predicament. For centuries now, she had been perfectly content to allow Robin, and the world for that matter, *believe* that Santa was responsible for Christmas. When in reality, it was every mother, every grandmother, every sister and aunt in the history of Christmas who made the magic what it was.

Starting with Mary herself.

"Oh, you think you are the reason Christmas is such a long lived celebration?" Mary practically growled at Robin.

"I would say we are near equals in that regard," Robin replied, barely masking the venom in his voice. "When was the last time you were where you said you were going to be when you said you were going to be there? At least I run on time!"

"Time? Time!" Mary scoffed. "It is my gift of *time* that allows *you* enough *time* to visit every household that celebrates. Without me, there would be no Christmas!"

Mary's eyes were as round as saucers. The audacity of it. Equals? Robin and Mary? She was the Queen of Winter and he was the Claus. They were on the same footing as Titania and Puck. As Galadriel and Samwise. Merlin and Wart. They were as equal in their gifts and responsibilities as Gloriana and Shakespeare.

She threw her head back and laughed. It was a bitter, resentful laugh. "When was the last time you baked a pie? Or wrapped a gift? When was the last time you counted every penny in the jar to see if there was enough money for more than socks?"

"I don't give them socks!" Robin snapped.

"That's the point, my Merry old Elf," Mary stalked forward until they were practically nose to nose. "Not just this holiday but *every* holiday. Mothers plan the festivities. Wives buy the groceries. Daughters wrap the presents. And you want a gold star for hammering a few nails and trimming garlands of lights? For tucking a few gifts under the tree? For the *delivery*? The postman is just as effective and far less trouble! And don't get me started on *this* holiday," Mary seethed.

"Thanksgiving? I thought you liked turkey," Robin said. The blatant confusion on his face sent Mary into a tailspin, spiraling into a rage.

"Don't be foolish. This holiday is the one where fathers get *all* the credit for making a turkey. They slice and dice and serve the best cuts to their favorite sons while most of them just watch a sports game and maybe, *MAYBE* drop a bird into a fry bin while tossing back the most despicable ales mankind has ever brewed.

"Meanwhile, Mother has been planning for weeks. Mother called the family and coordinated travel plans. She has prepared the stuffing and cut the root vegetables. She has rolled out the dough and whipped the cream. Even if she hasn't crafted everything on the table by hand, she still brought it all *together*. Its the women folk who spend the time to make the magic possible."

Mary was seething. The younger generations got it. Millennials and Gen Z, even some Alphas just understood. They hosted a Friendsgiving where everyone contributed and the kinship outweighed the significance of a single day. No one would be left out in the cold. No one would feel like they had to do it all alone only to receive grief when some obnoxious uncle, who hadn't bothered to even bring a bottle of wine, thought the bird was *dry*.

Wasn't kinship the entire point of the holiday in the first place? Community and friendship of a shared meal.

Robin was quiet for a long moment. She had to give him credit for listening and considering her words. Deep down, Robin had always been a good man. But she was not going to give him the reins to their story any longer.

Mary had been drafted into obscurity over the centuries. Her name invoked as the loving wife, resigned to making cookies and doting on Santa after a hard day's work. Which could not be further from the truth.

"You're right," Robin said, his righteous anger abandoned. "But neither will there be a Christmas without me. We need each other, my queen."

"What are we even talking about?" Mary asked.

"I really don't know," Robin said quietly.

Mary studied him closely. The twinkle of his eyes was muted to a glimmer. His cheerful cherub smile was a thin grimace. His sturdy frame had somehow folded in, smaller than she had ever seen him.

Mary was essential for Christmas to be successful, and he knew it. There was no Christmas without Mary. But he was right too. There was no Christmas without the Claus.

Every mother is a Christmas, every father is a Kringle.

They did need each other to fulfill their long ago bargain. He could hang his lights and deliver presents. Mary would bake her cookies and paint the winter in her special kind of wonder.

Time would stand still for her so that he could fly. It would take the two of them together to bring about the magic.

"Yes, of course," Mary relented. "It does take two to make the magic work. But you picked…"

He had picked *her.*

Mary was indignant at best, but under it all, she was hurt. Not because she had any romantic feelings for Robin or twisted propriety regarding the creatures of winter. But because Phyrne was a truly nasty person with cruelty in her heart.

Mary had a wicked side, to be certain, but her heart

weighed towards Chaotic Good. Mary's heart was loving and true, in her own way. She would never have been given her glacial gifts all those years ago if she hadn't been.

Echoes of their long history as the Claus and Winter Queen flitted across Robin's eyes. For the briefest of moments, understanding washed over Robin's face, and his features softened.

Mary could have none of that. She wouldn't allow him to make her vulnerable. He didn't get to see her hurt as if it belonged to him. Not today. Not any day.

"Oh, pish posh. I suppose it matters not a wink, does it?" She shifted in her seat as she fluffed snowy hair over her shoulder.

"Mary..." Robin began, extending a hand to her. She waved him off and stood without assistance before she stormed from his home.

She walked briskly across the quiet road and entered through her front door. She slouched out of her apple green coat, hanging it on the hook before she turned toward the kitchen ready to set her broken heart in order.

The kitchen... was spotless.

But who had cleaned it up?

The hardwood had been mopped and polished, not a spec of glass or debris. The center island had been washed, the glass swept clear.

Baking soda was a particularly difficult substance to remove once it coated a surface. Without a deep scrubbing it might linger in crevices for weeks. But the filmy residue was nowhere to be found.

Mary circled the kitchen, carefully examining every nook and cranny. Her spices had been returned to her cupboard, organized alphabetically. Her dishes from breakfast, which had been waiting for her in the sink, were gone. Cleaned and dried, each plate shelved on the display rack below the glassware.

On the center island, bundled in a willow reed basket, were all the ingredients Mary needed for her extra special cookies. Beside it, resting in wax paper and cheesecloth, tied with a spindle of twine was a new quart of farm fresh butter. A brown paper package of granulated raw sugar was tucked tightly beside a sack of freshly milled flour. A small silver tin of nutmeg was stacked on top of a matching tin of powdered cinnamon.

Her polished kettle whistled shrilly just as she stepped onto her shining hardwood floors. She hustled to the stove to douse the fire. A ceramic mug she recognized as belonging to Robin waited, a silk bag stuffed with honey and chamomile tea patiently prepared from his private reserves.

And then she knew.

His Brownies had done this. Not the chocolate kind of brownie. Robin's personal pixie minions, tiny elves no bigger than an apple who held a penchant for clean and orderly homes. The fairy tale creatures famously responsible for all the gift making and toys in the world had done this.

Robin had done this.

Mary swallowed the lump in her throat and wiped at her watery eyes. The silly things betrayed her as tears broke free of the dam holding back everything she felt. An emotional tempest roared through her, overwhelming her sense of here and now.

There was a small *thump*. Mary turned to find a rolling pin had joined the basket of ingredients. A cheerful red bow and brown paper tag looped around its middle. Mary fingered the tag.

"From the fires of Hekla for a taste of home. I'm sorry. —R."

The dark obsidian caught the light and shimmered like the northern lights. The handles were carved of cedar wood, tiny reindeer chasing one another around their hilt.

It wasn't her mother's moonstone crystal rolling pin, but it had been made in the heart of Robin's domain. An offering of a truce if she had ever seen one. A better apology even than his Brownie house elves, who had cleaned her home more thoroughly than even she could.

Strange how they knew exactly what she needed for her famous cookies.

It was bad manners to acknowledge the Brownies directly. Thanking them implied a debt, a debt which must be paid. But a general expression of gratitude… Well, no one would know who exactly she was thanking. It could be anybody.

"Thank you," Mary whispered.

CHAPTER FOURTEEN

Turkey & Tamales

Mary baked late into the night, resting only long enough for the oven to work its fiery magic. She had enough cookies to blanket her entire block with personalized boxes by midnight. Magic free. Mostly.

Satisfied with her accomplishment, she'd dropped into her bed and sank into a deep and peaceful sleep. She dreamed of volcanoes, reindeer, and sleigh rides.

It was early, the light just beginning to glow through her windows. She made a leisurely effort at clothes before heading back downstairs to find her kitchen once again spotless. *Who knew Robin's little elves were so tidy?* She turned the kettle to high and waited, preparing her morning tea from ceramic jugs full of loose leaves. An aromatic English Breakfast, lavender, and a dash of vanilla went into a silk pouch she tied shut with a swish of her finger. The tea was for herself, and magic was never against the rules in her kitchen.

The water had just started to boil when the screaming started.

It shattered the quiet of the early morning hours like a banshee war cry. Mary shut off the fire under the kettle and hurried outside to see what all the fuss was all about.

Phyrne, in her usual pink silk robe that did absolutely nothing to conceal anything, stood in the middle of her yard. She shrieked and jumped this way and that as if bounced by an invisible force. Her wailing summoned half the neighborhood.

The turkeys had come to town.

Every inch of Phyrne's frostbitten lawn was covered with feathered friends. At least a hundred birds of various sizes and ages had positively flocked to Washington Street. Every last one of them nestled in the Nesbitt yard.

They roosted in the branches of Phyrne's birch tree, the poor topiary strangled by Christmas lights. Some were perched on the roof of her hideous beige sedan, which was parked in the driveway and not the double-garage for unknown reasons. Their four clawed toes scratched the finish off the vehicle's paint.

Mary was positively delighted.

She clapped a hand over her mouth to keep from giving herself away as more neighbors poured onto the street. Some were already in their work clothes, some were still in their pajamas. They began congregating, clumping in groups to point in alarm or whispering behind cupped palms. Everyone was simply thankful the fowl flock of butter balls were not in *their* yard, opting to roost exclusively in Mrs. Nesbitt's yard.

How in the world did that happen?

Just lucky, they supposed.

Mary snorted.

"Turkeys!" Phyrne was screaming into a cell phone now. "There are wild turkeys… everywhere!" There was a brief pause while Phyrne listened to whoever was on the receiving end of her call. "No, you don't understand. They are *EVERYWHERE!*"

"Funny, isn't it?" Robin said casually. He'd steered clear of his own house, keeping as far away from Phyrne and the turkeys as possible. He'd meandered straight into Mary's driveway.

"What's that?" Mary asked.

"Wild turkeys don't usually favor this street."

"I hadn't noticed," Mary commented. "Strange creatures, turkeys. They like to nest in places that offer them the most protection. Like trees and bushes. As far as possible from bothersome predators."

"I'm sure they do," Robin agreed, arms crossed and eyes twinkling with amusement. A smirk tugged at his rugged mouth. For some reason, it made Mary scowl.

"I find birds go where they please," Mary said hotly.

"Of course, my queen."

"I told you to stop calling me that."

"Yes, my queen."

Phyrne was screaming into her phone. "If you don't come and contain them, I'm within my right as a property owner to handle things myself! I promise, there will not be a happy ending for these birds!"

Mary was certain they heard her the next county over. She rolled her eyes, stalking across the road.

"Where are you going?" Robin asked.

"To save the turkeys, of course," Mary huffed. If Phyrne had her way with the turkeys, they'd all end up in ovens. Maybe Mary should make amends. She'd had her fun but she would be quite cross if Phyrne hurt any of the birds for her practical joke.

It took Mary an hour to coax Phyrne off her murderous rampage with the turkeys. Animal control had come, but by then, most of of the pecking poultry had vanished. A lone Gobbler had strutted about in her flower beds scratching and throwing dirt until Mrs. Nesbitt had nearly had an aneurysm. Animal control had captured the fowl tempered creature to release somewhere far far away from the neighborhood.

Phyrne had then spent the remaining time screaming at Mary, accusing her of seducing the birds into her yard. Which was technically correct. Without any proof, rational minds prevailed and her husband had finally come to claim her, ushering Phyrne back into their home to recover from the trauma.

The whole ordeal had left Mary cross. The momentary delight she had in the initial moments had worn thin the longer Phyrne took to be reasonable. Why was that woman so stubborn?

Rather than dwell on insufferable nincompoops, Mary sighed and got to work on the lights she'd purchased from the hardware store. Surely imitation lighting was bound to bring that twinkle back to her eye, right? Maybe. She wasn't sure. She had *never* used string lights before, but she would try anyway.

Chuck-the-tool-man from the hardware store had promised it was easy to string the new state of the art light strings she had purchased. Of course, he has also suggested her grandchildren might be of assistance. Unfortunately, Mary didn't have any grandchildren.

Somehow, between the hardware store and unboxing her garlands of lights… Mary had managed to thoroughly tangle the fifteen boxes of extremely long rope lights into an unimaginable heaping ball of uselessness. She'd thrown them down in a fit and stormed into her basement to find other decorative accoutrements.

Sequestered in the murky light of her basement, Mary began to dig through boxes. She was in a dark mood with an even fouler temper. She knew the only way to truly banish the darkness was to chase it away. So, she searched for silver bells.

Not just any bells. These bells had been smelted and beaten into their polished silver shapes by Mary's mentor, Nikolaus. He had been an apothecary in her village, many many moons ago. The bells were the size of a large cat and had been etched with an assortment of reindeer, holly, and mistletoe, along with his professional signet marking him as a healer.

She hadn't seen or used them in so long she'd forgotten where she left them. So, she was searching for her silver bells. She found them in a bin labeled *weapons*, for reasons she couldn't recall. The bin produced no weapons of any kind, but actually held a random assortment of bedding inside. The bells had been neatly folded inside several of the blankets. Mary hoisted the entire box up the rickety old steps, thumping the worn cardboard down on the kitchen island.

She had just dug out the last of the five giant bells when there was a firm knock on her door. She let the bells stand, their tongues still as she answered the door.

"Mary Christmas!" three small voices piped over her frustration.

The three musketeers, Magdelena, Jax, and Carlos were waiting patiently at the foot of Mary's porch. Jax was pulling a red Radio Flyers wagon laden with cardboard boxes and folded towels. The other two children were guarding the sides to make sure the boxes didn't tip.

Each child was bundled up in their own preferred colors. Magdelena had a puffy Barbie pink parka with matching hat, scarf, and finger mittens. Her middle brother Carlos had a bright orange coat of similar style to his sister without any labeling. Just warmth and color enough to spot him in a crowd.

The oldest, Jax, wore a Miles Morales Spider coat, black with red piping and accents. His gloves and boots matched, his wild black hair untamed without any cap. Their personalities shined in their choices. Mary really loved children. There was so much potential in every choice.

"Good afternoon, children. How are we today?" Mary

asked, dusting off invisible dirt from her hands as she came to let them in the gate with their wagon.

"Good afternoon," Jax said. "Our mama says we are to offer our help cleaning up your yard to thank you for the cookies."

"Did she?" Mary asked with amusement.

"And for the toys!" Magdelena insisted. "Don't forget the toys!"

"Hush, *niña*! If she really is Mrs. Claus, do you want her to know you are really wicked and only here for the toys?" Jax chided his sister.

Mary smiled.

"Wicked children are my favorite," she said. The children's eyes went wide. "But of course only if they pledge to never be wicked for their mothers."

The three hooligans nodded solemnly.

"Mama says we are to help with your chores," Magdelena reminded them. Her brothers scowled, clearly disgruntled with the order.

"She sent us with tamales too," Carlos said shyly, unfolding the first wrapped towel to reveal foil wrapped tamales.

"Did she?" Mary asked with excitement. "Consider me intrigued."

She stepped forward and inhaled deeply. She smelled

rotisserie chicken and spices wrapped in hand folded masa and corn husks. Her mouth began to water. Mary couldn't remember the last time she'd had a quality tamale. She'd been remorseful she didn't get a taste of the *pozole* she'd made for their family. But one of Selena's tamales might just make up for it.

"Oh, yes! Those will be just delightful," Mary said with a swoon.

"Mama never makes tamales for…" Jax couldn't quite find the words.

"For stuffy old women who look like me?" Mary asked with a smile. "Why would she? You tell your mama thank you."

"We promise!" Magdelena swore.

"Excellent," Mary beamed, clapping her hands in delight.

"Are you going to make us work?" Jax asked, an edge of bitterness to his voice.

Mary crossed her arms and looked at the children pensively. She despised untangling Christmas lights. She'd never had to use them before, relying entirely on her magic to set her house glittering with merriment. But she was a woman of principle, and she had given her word. No magic.

Plus, she had fifteen boxes she'd bought and paid for.

Might as well use them.

Sadly, hers were as twisted as a Gordian Knott. Slicing through them with a saber would prove impractical. She was ready to try anything else until she calmed enough not to set the house on fire.And hadn't that nice man, what was his name? Chuck-from-the-hardware-store. Chuck had told her he'd used his grandchildren to organize his lights. Mary didn't have grandchildren, but she did have little neighbors.

Little neighbors who owed her a favor. And tamales. Mary practically purred.

"Does anyone have... what's the little box with the screen called?"

"A phone?" Jax asked. *How did this woman not know what a phone was?* was implied with his tone of disgust.

Mary grinned. "Well, this nice man at the store sold me boxes of lights. I've never used them before, but I believe you download an application to your phone—"

"It's just called an app," Jax said.

"Yes, of course. An *app*. Do you have one?" Mary asked. Jax dug in his pocket and held up his phone. It had a red and black Deadpool case with a gushing wound pop-it in the middle. Mary tilted her head. "Excellent! Jax is in charge of lights."

"Me?" Jax asked.

"Yes, you can untangle that mess. If I like your work I'll let you and the little… app-phone control the music. I haven't the foggiest on how an app-phone moves light. So, you're in charge."

Jax groaned but set to work untangling the strands.

"And you two," she turned to remaining siblings. "I have it on good authority that Santa will not come to this street unless we banish the wicked. I have just the magic tools to do it, but I need strong helpers. Any volunteers?"

Magdelena and Carlos shot their hands into the air, quick to volunteer.

"Perfect! Why don't I put the tamales inside while you three get started on the lights? I'll make us some cocoa. When you're done with the lights the real fun can begin."

By the time Mary returned with the cocoa, the children had untangled the messy web she had made and organized them into twelve neatly coiled piles. She gave each of them a steaming mug, but not too hot as to burn little tongues. They sipped merrily at their treat, wrapping cold fingers firmly around the ceramic mugs as Mary set the tray aside.

"Thank you, Mary Christmas," Magdelena said.

"You can just call me Mary if you like," she said. "Now, for our next task."

Jax and Carlos cringed. They knew they'd gotten off easy

with the lights. "Is it an outside task? Because it's getting late. Magdelena has a bedtime," Jax said.

"Do not! I'm a big girl like you and Carlos!"

"Well, this one is outdoors, but it is an opportunity to be a little bit naughty without getting on the naughty list." They all shifted in their seats, excitement humming between them. "Any takers?"

Three hands shot into the air.

"Delightful!" Mary looked back at where the silver bells glittered. Their polished handles and arching domes just begged to be rang. "Everyone grab a bell."

CHAPTER FIFTEEN

Santa

Robin finished bending the wire mesh of his current craft to his will. Not using magic, as he had agreed, was proving difficult. He had dozens of cuts on his hands and new calluses that hadn't been there for centuries.

But he would bend all of these woodland winter creatures into their beautiful sculpted forms if it killed him. He stood, digging his fists into his lower back. It was a futile attempt to relieve the ache.

A disharmonious peel of silver bells began chiming at irregular intervals. The voices of three small children bellowed into the cacophony of noise. "Angels we have heard on high!"

Robin dropped his wire mesh art project and stalked to

the garage wall. He thumped the button that would send the garage door inching upward.

"Sweetly singing o'er the plains. And the mountains in reply…"

The door slowly revealed his red beast of a truck… and children. The three Ortiz children marched up and down the sidewalk in front of his house. Each child clanged a giant silver bell the size of basketballs as they belted out Christmas carols. Badly.

"What in all that is holy?" Robin growled low in his throat.

Bing-Bong! Bing-Bong-GONG! There was no rhythm to the bells at all. "Echoing their joyous strains! Glo—"

"Hey!" he barked at the children, loud enough that they startled to a stop. "What do you think you are doing?"

"Mrs. Claus told us Santa wouldn't bring us any presents unless we chased the dark and wicked away," little Magdelena declared.

"She said we had to ring these bells to chase away evil," Carlos confirmed.

"Our mom said we had to help Mary Christmas," Jax said with a suffering sigh. "This is what she told us to do."

Robin's eyes caught on Mary Christmas. Pleased as punch she stood at her front window sipping from her favorite cerulean mug, watching. Waiting. She brought the mug to her lips and grinned, steam billowing around her face and fogging the window. Robin touched his fingers to his forehead and saluted her.

"Did Mary tell you who *I* am?" Robin asked in hushed tones. The children stopped ringing their bells and looked over their shoulders as if they could see her. Mary had abandoned her vigil, having accomplished her goal of annoying him.

Robin grinned. It was good she couldn't quite see him anymore.

"Who are you, mister?" The littlest, Magdelena, asked. She was bundled up snugly in a pink parka and matching knitted cap with a pom on top. It accentuated the rich dark colors of her brown eyes and raven hair. Her brother's attention returned to Robin at the question.

"I'm Santa Claus," He said, a secretive twinkle in his eye as he tapped his finger against the side of his nose.

"Bullshit!" Jax said.

"*Mano!*" Magdelena and Carlos cried in unison.

"What? First, the old lady is Mrs. Claus. Now this guys Santa? Do they look married to you?"

"You don't look like Santa," Carlos reluctantly agreed.

"There. See. He doesn't even look like Santa." Jax crossed his arms over his chest in an effort to look cool and unimpressed. It failed miserably with the giant silver bell dangling from his hand and the tell tale Spider Man hoodie and shoes he was reluctant to let go of. Robin hoped he held on to that innocence a little longer.

"Does she look like Mrs. Claus?" Robin smiled at them.

"Yes," all three chimed in enthusiastic unison.

"Yes, I suppose she does," Robin chuckled. It brought him a great deal of joy that these children saw the whimsical version of Mary Christmas. They accepted as *fact* that she was Mrs. Claus and could maybe put in a good word for them.

"Are you really Santa?" Carlos asked.

He was fully aware what they saw when they looked at him. A middle aged man with more brown hair than white. Torn jeans and a faded flannel shirt stuffed under a corduroy and sheepskin coat. Robin looked more like a lumberjack or an insufferable hipster than Santa these days.

"Do you still want that *'Lucky Doug Robot'* set?" Robin asked casually. Carlos nodded emphatically. "How about you, Jax? I thought you were really set on having that *'Minecraft: the Art of Drawing'* book."

"How he know what we want?" Carlos asked.

"Me, Santa! Guess mine!" Magdelena begged.

"Oh, you, little miss. You've been so good this year," Robin began, getting down on one knee to face her eye to eye. Her brother's scoffed. "She *has* been good. Two older brothers tormenting her and she still managed to take out the trash for you both on three separate occasions even though it's *your* shared responsibility."

"Dude, no way!" Jax exclaimed. "*¿Cómo sabe lo que dijo mamá?*"

"*Lo sé todo, chico*," Robin replied calmly. The boys eyes became saucers.

"Hey, when you learn to speak Spanish?" Jax demanded.

"He's Santa, duh!" Magdelena declared. "Santa speaks every language."

Robin grinned. "Magdelena, you want roller blades. And a helmet, of course. I'm inclined to give them to you, but I need a favor first."

Magdelena, Jax, and Carlos were excellent conspirators as Robin made his plan. He knew his Halloween display had made Mary see red with all the inflatable decorations. He'd put special care into selecting the Christmas ones he planned on deploying at a later date. Maybe in Phyrne's yard if she would let him.

In the meantime, though, he thought it might be great fun to walk the neighborhood in a different inflated costumes, just to see how far he could take it. They were, of course, built for a man of his stature. They wouldn't fit the children at all.

The no magic rule was only for decorations, he decided. They never set any specific agreement for costumes and frivolity. Robin set his finger against his nose and winked at the children. The gingerbread shrank to the size of a six-year-old, the snowman to the size of eight-year-old. For Jax, it looked like he was riding an inflatable reindeer, miniature elf legs draped over the sides and leaving his arms free. Robin kept the adult sized awkward looking stuffed turkey for himself. They were giggling as they pulled on their costumes, Robin and Jax helping the little ones adjust the Velcro to fit.

"Magdelena, I think you should take lead," Robin suggested. "And you boys follow your sister. I'll stay in the back."

The children obediently lined up, giant silver bells in their hands clanging with every step. "And let's keep the bells quiet until we get to her driveway, okay?"

The inflatable menagerie proceeded down the driveway with Magdelena leading the little quartet. Robin marched them straight across the road where they tread in place, face to face with the red sequin capped gargoyles. Mary had added thick red ribbons twining through the posts since the last time he'd paid them any mind. He chuckled.

"Everyone ready?" He called from the back of the line. The children looked over their shoulders and nodded.

"Ok... One, two, three!"

They sang, on key, ringing the bells in time as they belted out "Jingle Bell Rock" in a lovely blend of voices. It mostly worked because children always sound sweet. The Ortiz children had rich voices full of warmth and love.

Robin hadn't noticed Mary sitting in a rocking chair on her front porch either, a cut glass of clear bubbling liquid and a slice of lime in her hands. He slowed his pace as the children angled near. Mary waited patiently, a cat ready to pounce on her prey. Robin was the only bird in the parade, and he was squarely in Mary's sights. He swallowed a lump. Perhaps he had been too hasty at returning her favors.

"Jingle bell chime, and jingle bell rhyme!" The children were practically shouting. *Oh no.* Robin waddled his overstuffed turkey closer.

At the same moment, Mary set down her beverage and began striding toward the lot of them. Jax noticed her first, his bell clanging off rhythm as he looked between Robin and Mary. Carlos noticed his brother then he noticed Mary. Magdelena was the last to stop singing, looking bewildered with a small crease between her brows as she considered her brothers.

"Why'd we stop singing?"

"Do you see the look on her face?" Jax hissed under his

breath.

Magdelena didn't seem to think there was anything wrong with Mary's expression, but the boys had more experience with the mom look. They kept a healthy distance as their little sister darted forward in her gingerbread inflatable and set her giant bell on the grass.

"We brought the bells back," Magdelena said, craning her head back to look up at Mary. Her cherubic face was tightly framed by the costume. She looked so much like a real little gingerbread that Mary suddenly started to laugh.

"Oh, well played, Mr. Goodfellow. Well played," Mary said.

Robin, wrapped in fat turkey polyvinyl, waited at the edge of the driveway. He was confident she wouldn't lose her temper on the children. He was less confident about his own safety in this exact moment.

Sensing a rising tension between the adults, Jax and Carlos sidled closer to the street, the snowman and reindeer puffs slowly deflating as their boots scrapped the fabric against the pavement.

"We thought you might enjoy some caroling, on key," Robin offered cautiously.

"Most definitely," Mary agreed.

There was a sharpness in the look she darted in his direction. He would have been skewered like a kabob if the dart had been real. But the warmth and delight she had for the Ortiz family reminded him she had a soft spot for innocent children. Always had and always would.

"Hey, Mrs. Christmas?" Jax said, setting down his bell and shuffling out of the reindeer onesie. "I think it's time for me to take the little ones home. Mama will be wondering where we are. Did we help enough?"

"Yes, of course. You performed beautifully," Mary beamed at them. "And thank you for untangling my lights. I'll be sure to report back to Santa what excellent helpers you were."

"He's right here!" Magdelena blurted, snatching Robins hand and dragging him into the yard. "How come you're not married to Santa?"

Mary gave Robin a look that would melt glacier ice caps. Robin had the decency to blush crimson, a tight smile as he waddled forward.

"Magdelena! You don't ask people why they aren't married," Jax scolded, stepping toward his sister. "Sorry. She's little and doesn't understand."

"Am not! I do too understand! I'm a big girl!" Magdelena protested.

"Yes you are, my dear one," Mary soothed, stooping to her level to look Magdelena in the eye. "And sometimes big girls will understand when they are much much older, don't you think?"

"I suppose," she grumbled. Magdelena studied them both for a long time. And then, as fast as any child who suddenly realized that Christmas was on the line she added, "Were we good enough? Do we still get presents?!"

"Of course," Robin assured her. "You all were so good."

Jax rolled his eyes, kicking aside the reindeer and helping Carlos unstuff himself from the snowman. "Come on, *hermana*. Mama will be wanting us home."

"Can I keep the gingerbread?" Magdelena asked. She was so stuffed into her inflatable, she had to turn her whole body to look between Robin and Mary. The effect was that she really was a little gingerbread.

"If your mama says yes, then of course," Robin said.

They made a sight, the Ortiz children walking home. Jax towing a wagon with Carlos and the little gingerbread. Robin couldn't help the grin that spread over his face.

"What do you possibly have to be so pleased about?" Mary snapped.

"What?" Robin was momentarily confused as he brought his attention back to Mary. Then he remembered he was wearing a ridiculous turkey inflatable and there were discarded bells and polyvinyls all over her yard. "Oh... I... was just thinking of the children," he hedged.

"Are you now?" Mary puffed a breath of misty air,

hands on hips.

"Yes," Robin said.

Mary glanced again down the street. Jax was lifting the little gingerbread out of the wagon. As soon as her feet touched the ground, Carlos towed the Radio Flyer away to be stored in the garage. They looked back as if sensing they were being watched and waved at Robin and Mary. Mary deflated.

"Yes, very well. For the children," Mary sighed in resignation.

"Although, we agreed no magic," he cautioned.

"I didn't use magic," Mary clapped back, fire returning to her temper. Robin swore internally. Not what he'd intended.

"You made them cookies. You told them you were Mrs. Claus," he said, softly.

"And you haven't, *Santa*? These damnable inflatables positively reek of *your* magic," she scolded, holding up the limp snowman as if it might bite her.

Robin stalled. Unsure how to proceed. He reached out to collect the melting fabricated snowman from her but Mary snatched it back.

"It was just a bit of fun," he said.

"For the record, I only confirmed their suspicions to give their mother a much needed reprieve. The woman was positively harried!" she called over her shoulder.

"How so?"

"Not that it's any of *your* business," Mary snapped, hands on hips. "I made the family dinner. A nice *pozole* soup. *And* I made them cookies. Perfectly normal everyday cookies. The children tidied their room and their mother got a peaceful moment to herself!"

Robin blinked several times, tipping his head in admiration. "That was very kind of you, my queen."

"I told you to stop calling me that. They will hear you."

Robin decidedly ignored her concern. "Somehow you managed to gift them all a little peace. Even the children. They won't soon forget it."

Mary sucked in a strained breath. She forcefully extended her hand, the snowman sagging in white folds of disappointment. "Please see to it these poly-vomit-inflatables find their way into the rubbish bin. I've grown quite tired of them." Without waiting for him, Mary spun on her heel and marched toward her front door in a huff.

Robin sighed, bending awkwardly to retrieve Rudolph and Frosty from the ground. He watched in silence as Mary retreated into her house. He waited for her to close her door before turning to waddle back to his own yard.

"You gave them something to believe in. That is a gift, my queen, one you may not understand. But it was a gift.

Thank you," he said to himself, hoping perhaps the words would reach her on the wind.

CHAPTER SIXTEEN

Mary Christmas

Mary wasn't sure why she had never thought about it before. Of course she could meddle in her neighbors affairs. Of course she could be a part of the solution. She was the Queen of Winter! Of course she could fix everything.

So, why did a little flea in her ear keep telling her she was out of her damned mind?

Enough with the inner voices. Mary was going to *do* something for every neighbor who needed it. She supposed a walk around the neighborhood was in order to see who needed what. She put on her apple green coat, pausing to appreciate its silk lining and warm alpaca wool overlay. She stepped outside and set out at a brisk pace.

Around the block it was about 50/50 whether homes had begun their decorating in earnest or not at all. Honestly, Mary didn't care one way or the other. She enjoyed herself, and that was really all that mattered. As the holidays got closer, she would wiggle her way into the lives of those who she found not participating. But for now, a walk.

"Mrs. Christmas, Mrs. Christmas!" the girl with the buddy holly glasses from the meeting called out. Today, she was wearing a pink "Girls Run the Galaxy" sweatshirt, a silhouette of a woman with her hair in twin buns on the back. She rushed down a set of steps from her xeriscaped yard. The home had one of the largest lots and was completely void of the hyper manicured lawns so many Americans adored. There were none of the overly pruned bushes that *some* neighbors, mainly Phyrne, were fond of.

Mary recalled when the family who owned the charming twin Victorian craftsman to her own had moved in. They'd immediately repurposed their once green grass into an edible garden and water conservative native plant beds for pollinators. They had a quaint hand painted sign alerting people that the overgrowth was intentional.

Of course there had been immediate blowback from certain neighbors, taking it so far as to involve the city council. The family had won their case with the loosey-goosey HOA, pointing to the climate crisis and water shortages. Now the hand painted sign had an official garden plaque from the city applauding their efforts in conservation and creativity. Mother and daughter even had their picture in the paper.

Phyrne had an absolute meltdown.

Mary consumed an absurd amount of popcorn that week as she enjoyed the show.

"Yes, my dear. What can I do for you?" Mary asked, closing the small gap between them.

"I was wondering if you might help me with my decorations?" She asked in a hopeful voice, both hands clasped in plea as she begged.

"Me?" Mary was a little taken aback. Not because she wasn't good at decorating—Mary was *excellent* at everything she did—but no one had ever asked her for that sort of help before. "You want me to help with your decorations?"

"Yes."

Mary looked around at the xeriscaped yard. On top of an old wheelbarrow turned planter box was a strange little green man in a brown tunic about three feet tall. His ears jutted out large enough to be bat wings. The girl had put a red stocking cap between the ears, the excessively long tail and white puffy pom dripped over his shoulder. In both three fingered hands, he held a light up sword in a warriors stance.

"I…." She wasn't sure how exactly to respond. "Is that an alien?"

"Him?" The girl turned. "That's Grogu. He's impaled the imperial forces of Christmas."

Mary tilted her head and looked again. A deflated Santa, Rudolph, and Frosty lay scattered about the yard. She spotted Robin's deflated Turkey she had dismembered too. In the picture the girl was painting, this strange little alien figure had defeated Christmas with his blade of light.

"I like it. Your idea?"

"Me and my mom." She nodded. "We're big Mandalorian fans."

"I see that," Mary said with a smile. She wasn't sure she fully understood what the girl was talking about. Mary had no idea what a Mandalorian might be, but she could get behind the little alien using a magical Force to disembowel a polyvinyl Santa.

"We don't really have extra money for decorating the yard like everyone at the meeting was saying," the girl admitted softly, digging her steel toed boot into the soft earth of her yard. "So, I went and found some decorations people were throwing away because they're torn or broken. Mr. Goodfellow gave me the inflatables. I staged them with Grogu. I thought maybe I could borrow your frogs?"

"My frogs?" Mary asked, bewildered. "What do frogs have to do with—"

"Grogu likes to eat them… in the show. He can't stop eating frogs. I thought some of your Halloween decorations would be a nice addition to the low-key vibe I'm going for."

She watched the girl with interest. She was in her teen years, mostly solitary as far as Mary could tell. She had never noticed any friend groups riding bikes or knocking on the door inviting her to go on an adventure. She gave Mary the overall impression she was sad, desperately trying to find a little joy in this season.

"It's just me and my mom these days," the girl was saying. "So Christmas is a little tight, but I wanted to participate."

Mary approached the girl and took both of her hands. They were nearly as cold as her own. The girl looked up at Mary with surprise. She responded with a warm and inviting smile.

"Your creativity is pure magic, child," Mary said. "Of course you can borrow the frogs."

"Really?" She bounced with anticipation and Mary

laughed.

"Really," Mary said conspiratorially. "Can you imagine the look on Mrs. Nesbitt's face when she notices the frogs in your display?"

The girl's smile broke into a grin of pure mischief, her eyes twinkling in the twilight. "Can you imagine her face if I win and demand everyone has to decorate with Star Wars next year?"

"Oh," Mary said, with a laugh. "I can imagine. Why don't you come visit me in an hour. I'll pack up those frogs for you."

"Thank you Miss Christmas. You're the best!" Without warning, the girl threw her arms around Mary in a firm embrace before running into her house.

Back in her garage, Mary shuffled through a box until she found what she was looking for. A dozen frogs in varying shapes and sizes, but all larger than a softball. Some were soft and pliable, some hard and carved of stone. All of them looked like they may have once have been people.

Because they once had been… people.

"Well, ladies and gentle-toads, I have a new purpose for you," Mary cooed to their lifeless forms. "It seems alien magicians find frogs to be a delicacy. Perhaps they're French. We're going to make a gift basket to welcome them to the neighborhood."

She could have sworn that some of the frogs shuddered as Mary got to work. She found a large grey and black basket with a flat bottom and a deep belly. She stuffed the base with an assortment of pinecones and set the frogs about on top like a bouquet. Then she added red and gold ribbons wrapping around the stem of the handle, tying a big fat bow around the belly of the basket. She stepped back to admire her work just as there was a knock on her front door.

"Be right there," Mary called out. She hefted the basket off the worktable with an *oomph* of effort. With all the stone frogs in one place the basket was much too heavy for any normal person to manage.

She frowned, considering her options. The decoration wasn't for *her* yard. Magically weighted stone frogs wouldn't break the rules. She twitched her nose as if she had an itch. A little flash of light circled around the basket and absorbed into the woven threads. The basket became no heavier than a loaf of bread.

"Much better," She said, nodding approval. She used her hip to unlatch the door that lead back into the house. She bumped it open with her butt as she made for the front door. A swish of her finger and that door swung open too.

"Wow, that's a lot of frogs," Robin commented dryly.

His infuriating capacity to be exactly where Mary didn't want him to be was unfathomable. She had the good sense to keep her sharp tongue behind her teeth when she spotted the young girl and her mother standing just behind him.

"I was just coming in from a walk and ran into these two. I had to see what they needed so many frogs for."

"None of your business," Mary snapped at him, but she turned a winning smile on the girl and her mother. "Here you are, my dear. All my frogs." She passed the basket to the young girl who grabbed it as if expecting a heavy load.

"Wow! They're so light!" she exclaimed, testing the weight by hefting it up and down ever so slightly.

"Oh, of course! Lights! Take three of these." Mary snatched several of the lights boxes the Otiz children had helped her organize off the porch. "I have more than I need. Your little alien friend simply must have a light show to go with his sword," Mary said.

"Wow! This will be perfect, won't it Mom?"

"This is very generous of you," her mother said. "My little rapscallion said she got some help with decorations. I just wanted to say thank you."

"My absolutely pleasure," Mary replied. "Do be gentle with the larger toads, will you? Especially the fat one. She gets moody if she gets too much sun."

The girl and her mother gave Mary a quizzical look as they retreated and made their way home. Robin turned on Mary the moment the family was out of ear shot.

"What are you up to, Mary?"

"Oh, what's it to you? Can't an old woman help a young girl when she calls for aid?"

"Yes, but you aren't any old woman," Robin countered.

"Careful, Robin Goodfellow. Lest I change my mind and turn you into one of my toads for talking too much."

"You really are letting her use the *Froskaprinsar*? What if she breaks a frog?"

"So what if she does? Every last one of them deserved their mortar fate. What's it to you? Shouldn't you be concerning yourself with Christmas and toy land? I hear my jolly old elf isn't holding up his end of our bargain."

"What does that mean?" Robin hissed, his stormy eyes narrowing to slits.

"It means that of all the streets in the world to miss, you could at least cover all the children in *this* neighborhood. Is that too much trouble?"

Robin gnashed his teeth at her. "I get every child who sends a wish. Every child on this block gets exactly what they need."

"Except that one," Mary said, pointed her finger at the girls back.

"Do you even know her name?" Robin asked through clenched teeth.

"It doesn't matter. You're not helping her, so I am," Mary scoffed. "Besides, I quite like the addition of my little toads. The frog Princes add just the right amount of… oh, what's the word? Oh. Yes. Magic."

Mary grinned as Robin finally noticed the display that the girl had arranged. The little Grogu alien, the light blade, the defeated polyvinyl inflatables. And now, the basket of stone frogs. It could not have been more perfect if Mary had designed it herself.

Robin sighed, shaking his head. "Her name is Jade."

"What?"

"The girl. Her name is Jade. Her mother is Sandra." Robin's mouth ticked up in a wry smirk.

"And just how do yo—" Mary stumbled, as Robin tapped the side of his nose and pointed at her. "Of course. You know when they're sleeping and when they're awake."

"When they've been bad and good," Robin said, a naughty twist of his full lips.

Mary rolled her eyes. "Goodness and badness is a matter of perspective," she declared.

"Lucky me, I get to be the perspective."

"You grade every child on a sliding scale anyway. Adults

too!" Mary said, waving a hand dismissively.

"As you wish, my queen."

"It's official. I'm going to teach the neighbors cat to vomit on your car," Mary warned him. Robin laughed. "You don't think I will?"

"Oh, I do. I do believe you will try. I will enjoy watching you try to train a Devon Rex cat do anything it doesn't want to do." Robin laughed all the way back into his house.

❅ ❅ ❅

Mary was in a foul mood the next morning. She had next to no time left to get her decorating done. And she had to do it all on her own. Without magic.

She really, *really,* was regretting that bargain.

She dragged her full sized sleigh and reindeer onto the lawn. Weaving between the decorations she had already set up had been a frustrating exercise in patience and logic.

"Need any help?" Robin's voice asked.

Mary was halfway up a ladder, a life-sized Santa in tow. She was lucky it was made of plastic, or she would never have been able to heft it up on her own. She sneered and turned back to her ladder. "I've been managing just fine without you. Why don't you see if your honey do-well

Mrs. Nesbitt needs anything?"

Mary clicked her tongue at Robin as she settled Santa on the roof. He fell over immediately and rolled on his rounded red belly. Mary huffed a frustrated breath. Robin sighed and began climbing up the ladder.

"Let me help you," he said, exasperated. He took the Santa from her hands and looked around for a good spot to secure him. There was none. "How do you plan to get him to fly?"

"How do you fly?" Mary countered.

Robin glowered, focusing intently on his work, tucking and tacking a plastic boot to the trim of her roof. She knew it ruffled his feathers that it was *her* magic that allowed Santa to be, well, Santa. And after she had stripped his privileges and powers last year over the debacle with the Red Cap Society… Well, he was lucky she left him any responsibility at all.

Oh, she'd give them back soon enough. Heaven knew she had enough to do this winter without delivering a billion gifts across the globe, but she'd make him sweat in the mean time. The neighborhood feud gave her plenty to torment him about for now.

"I thought we agreed no magic for the decorations this year. For obvious reasons," Robin said, standing to his full height with a knowing look as he shoved his hands in his pockets and examined his work.

"I haven't been using magic!" Mary flung her hands up in frustration. A stiff breeze swelled in response to her anger. It sent Santa flying into a bush despite Robins efforts to secure it.

A chuckle strangled itself in Robins throat. She whipped her icy glare to his face. His jaw was clenched tight, a muscle feathering as he schooled his features into a neutral countenance. It did nothing to mask the glitter of amusement in his blue eyes.

Mary crossed her arms over her chest sourly, glaring at the reindeer, sleigh, and Santa—the real one *and* the plastic one. There had to be a way to make them fly that didn't involve magic. Something mundane and practical that regular everyday people might use. How *did* normal people make anything fly? It might as well be magic as far as Mary Christmas was concerned.

Well, she'd figure something out.

"Excuse me," Phyrne said from the foot of Mary's driveway.

"Oh, for heavens sake. What does she want?" Mary muttered under her breath.

"Probably to give you another letter of condemnation. It was you who killed her lawn, wasn't it?" Robin goaded.

"I haven't the faintest idea what you're talking about,"

Mary replied, making for the ladder. Robin stopped her with a gentle but firm hand on her elbow.

"I'll go first. Just in case," he said with a wink.

Mary was half inclined to kick the ladder free, if it wouldn't make it difficult to explain herself. Sadly such theatrics would only extend the amount of time she would have to deal with her meddlesome neighbor. *Neighbors.* Plural. Mary waited until Robin made it to the foot of the ladder, bracing his boots on either side and resting strong hands against the rungs.

"Okay, your turn," Robin called to her.

Phyrne was waiting for her by the time Mary's first foot hit the grass. Today, the woman wore a sheath dress right out of the *Mommy Dearest* collection, a sour shade of yellow that did absolutely nothing for Phyrne's ruddy complexion.

"I hate to be the flea in your ear," Phyrne said in her honeyed rasp, "but if that sleigh or reindeer were to fall on anyone, well the consequences for gross negligence could be severe."

Mary took her time, dramatically looking up the length of ladder. She obviously hadn't even succeeded at getting the damned things up there. What exactly did this woman object to? Mary took her time dragging her attention back to Phyrne. Couldn't she see that this was a work in progress? Did she truly take delight in stealing peoples joy before it had even started?

"I know last year, and the year before that, you had these… decorations… on your roof. But I just wanted to caution you. They will have to come down as soon as the New Year is over, you know. Community standards and all. Winter here can be precarious, I wouldn't want you to injure yourself getting them down again," Phyrne went on.

Robin snorted, and Mary stepped on his booted foot. She took satisfaction in his muted groan. She'd hit the arch just right to cause pain but not break it. A small part of her wished she had, just a tiny little fracture.

"Of course, Phyrne," Mary finally managed to say, her voice as cold as iron. "Wouldn't dream of leaving my lights up past the new year."

Mary would leave them up for the next 365 days just to make a point now.

"Well. Good luck on Thanksgiving. Is your family coming to visit?"

Mary's lips thinned. "I haven't got any family to visit."

"Oh, that is so *sad* to hear," Phyrne bleated. "Well, at least they won't have to navigate this hazardous walkway." Mary rolled her eyes, frost cracking beneath her feet. Robin cleared his throat, and she reined in the rage building in her veins before she made a permanent ice sculpture out of Phyrne.

"I'm making a meal for Mr. Crabtree," Mary replied firmly.

"Mr. Crabtree?" Phyrne and Robin squawked at the same time.

"Yes. Cyrus was the one who enlightened me about the Three Sisters," Mary said sweetly. Phyrne's eyes darted toward the dancing trio and cringed. "Of course I'd make him dinner to say thank you."

"The Three..." Phyrne seemed to catch herself. "Of course, that's what neighbors are for." Phyrne smiled tightlipped, turning on her heal and stalking away.

"Mr. Crabtree?" Robin repeated.

"And why shouldn't I?" Mary asked hotly. "Two old fuddy-duddies who haven't a reason to celebrate a turkey, why shouldn't we have dinner?"

"I thought we always had dinner for Thanksgiving."

"Well, don't get your candy cane in a knot. You can join us too," Mary waved a dismissive hand. "Now, leave me alone while I ponder how to make this reindeer fly."

Robin stood still as stone for several heartbeats before bowing his head formally.

"Yes, my queen." He stalked away as hot tempered as Phyrne.

It wasn't like Thanksgiving was *her* holiday. Or his, for

that matter. She didn't really do feasting with anyone anymore, but that wasn't something small minded folk like Phyrne would ever understand, though Robin should have. Mary didn't understand the fuss.

She turned back and stared at her plastic Santa and toppled over reindeer and glowered. She needed to clear her head. She abandoned her project and started for the gate. As before, a walk around the block was bound to do it.

She hoped.

CHAPTER SEVENTEEN

Reindeer Fly

It was the night before Thanksgiving, and Mary noticed a decided uptick of neighbors on ladders. They were stringing lights along their rooflines as she walked around the block. It seemed every house in the neighborhood had finally taken the challenge seriously, even more so than usual.

Team Nesbitt chose to covered their homes in white everything. Thousands of lights glowing up and down sidewalks like runway beacons. Team Christmas burst with a rainbow of colors as though the Keebler Elves themselves had festooned everything in fairy dust. The entire neighborhood had forgotten why they were feuding in the first place, but everyone was equally determined to win whatever the battle was.

It delighted Mary to her very core.

While everyone had begun the decorating in earnest, she found a great many of them had utilized the inflatable decorations she had been so hung up on for Halloween. Some went with the more traditional winter staples: a snowman in a top hat with holly berries and presents in their arms, foxes in stocking caps, and even an inflatable gingerbread archway.

One house had thrown theme completely to the wind, a Jack Skellington and sleigh had been paired with a wooden Grinch cutout climbing the brick chimney and tugging on a light strand. Mary snorted when she saw the dinosaur riding Santa tucked under the awning alongside a Griswold station wagon and tree puttering nearby.

It was midday, so every inflatable was in sagging globules like a crime scene outline. But she could make out their intended shapes and found they didn't bother her as much as they had at Halloween.

Perhaps she had been too quick to judge. Or perhaps she had unfairly judged because Robin Goodfellow had been the one to initiate the polyvinyl chloride obsession. She supposed it was just the time they lived in, and without magic, how was one supposed to craft a magical wonderland? Humanity was at a disadvantage, and it was unfair of her to hold it against them. They had used the tools at their disposal, and she promised to not judge them. Mostly.

Phyrne's house was an execution in precision, if not imagination. The corded lights were strung as tight as a facelift. Her poor birch trees were strangled by so many wires it was a wonder they hadn't fallen over from carbon dioxide deprivation. Strands of blue icicle strands the length of a short bladed sword pierced down from the eaves in violent defiance.

Mary laughed. Glittering white lights and blue blades would not be enough to win this year's coveted *best of* status. She would vote for the alien and the light blade first.

After her walk, Mary spent the remainder of the day fussing over her own house. She had found clever ways to leave a number of the Halloween decorations exactly where they were only to repurpose them for Christmas.

Rather than eliminating the spooky and macabre entirely, Mary had bedecked them in bows of holly and ribbons of red and gold. The ghosts had been repurposed into a terrifying impersonation of Jacob Marley and Ebenezer Scrooge as the ghost of Christmas haunting the tiny stone graveyard in rattling chains. She made sure to add silver and white glitter to the chains so she could honestly say it was a Christmas decoration. And of course, the gargoyles she had already added little festive gnome hats in a variety of colors. She'd even spared one hat for Ebenezer.

While the witch hats had gone into the cauldron to support the glass ornaments for her festive cauldron bubbles, the witches themselves had transformed into the Three Sisters. She was decidedly pleased with the sisters.

Mr. Crabtree had been positively enchanted when he saw them dancing behind the cauldron, his eyes filling with tears. Cyrus had stayed and admired them for nearly an hour before disappearing down the street. He returned five minutes after and gifted Mary with a wooden carving of a Queen Bee he had whittled himself. It had quickly replaced her front door wreath. And it would stay there for the rest of always

The lights twined exactly as they had before, only instead of purple, orange, and slime green, they glowed with the red, white, and green of the forrest. The Ortiz children had been critical in helping her detangle the speedway lengths of electrical ropes. Now, every spare surface that could be was covered with glittering jeweled lights. Jax had been instrumental in choosing the color coordination theme. He had timed it for her from his phone—with his mother's permission of course.

But the crowning glory of Mary's decorating prowess had always been her life sized sleigh, complete with eight reindeer and a lifelike Santa. Every year, Santa and his reindeer were frozen in take off positions on her roof.

And every year previously, she had used magic.

She still didn't have a clue how the hell she was going to do it this year. Getting the sleigh and reindeer up there without her magical gifts was going to be tricky, at best. Getting them to *stay* up there was going to be an act of willpower and fortitude. Yesterday had been evidence enough of that.

There were a lot of angles on her roof, the steep Victorian slopes were going to make things difficult. She wondered if she *should* call Robin back. Maybe she could offer him a mulligan if he helped her. He had given her that beautiful rolling pin as an apology, after all.

Maybe they could go back to frenemies. With a nonchalant twist, Mary pretended to stretch out a stiff back so she could see what Robin was working on in his front yard.

His current project was wrestling with a wire mesh and pliers. From the grunting and swearing under his breath, it was not going as well as he hoped. Good. Let him struggle. It was his bright idea not to use magic. *Fool.*

Mary returned to her own task and hauled her plastic

ladder upright, bracing it against the lowest roofline she could reach. First order of business would be to get the darn reindeer up. See if it was even possible to make them fly.

Without magic.

She growled.

"Evening, Miss Christmas," a masculine voice greeted.

A man with kind brown eyes smiled and waved from the edge of the driveway. David Bly was the widower who lived next door to her. He hadn't lost his spark for life, though it had been a very near thing after his wife died. Not long after, his only daughter had left for college. He had been alone ever since.

"Good evening to you, David," Mary greeted him, willing the ice out of her voice. "How's your daughter, Zoë?"

Shadows danced across David's face, his smile fading. Mary kicked herself for even brining his daughter up. He had lost so much already.

"She's great. Happy as can be at her job. It's her whole world at the moment. She lives on the East coast now." Only an imbecile would hear his words and not his voice. David was in pain, an ache that couldn't be soothed. Come to think of it, Mary had not seen the absent girl in some time. She wondered what had become of her that she never returned home. A problem for another day.

A gentle nudge to his knee had David smiling again. Practically sitting on his feet was his black bear of a dog, Pirate. She was an aging flat-coated retriever, tender and fierce as a lion. David's family protector for nearly fifteen years. Her muzzle and paws were silvery grey, a fine match to David's weathered coloring.

"I hear Mrs. Nesbitt called in the troops. We're all supposed to decorate or die," David changed the subject smoothly.

Mary snorted. "That's the polite summary of events."

"Are those life-sized reindeer?"

"Well, you can't have a half-sized reindeer, now can you? The babies are quite unmanageable. They simply won't be tamed," Mary scoffed, as though it was common knowledge. Mary often forgot she wasn't entirely human.

"Need any help?" David offered.

Well, of course she needed help, but was it a violation of her terms of agreement with Robin? Was she unfairly influencing her neighbors? She had, after all, already bent the rules with the Ortiz children. Would soliciting help from the kindly widower be cheating at their little game?

No, by Christmas. It certainly was *not* cheating. David Bly was a good man offering his sweet old neighbor some help with her holiday decorations. Just like he sometimes shoveled her walkway in January. He didn't know she was perfectly capable of making it snow anywhere but her walkway if she chose.

"Can you make a reindeer fly?" Mary asked.

David scratched his head, his hand tousling his chocolate and silver hair. He was starting to look more and more like Santa, even more than Robin did at present. Which she hadn't realized annoyed her until just this moment. There was something perfectly respectable about a man in a beard. If a man earned his white stripes and laugh lines through acts of kindness, then so be it. Mary would have to tease Robin until he indulged her and grew a beard for Christmas.

Pirate nudged David's leg again. He rubbed behind her fluffy ear. "All right, all right. Pirate's fussy this evening. She's not ready for the cold yet. Her old paws don't like the icy sidewalks. Let me get her inside, and we'll see what we can come up with."

David was gone for about ten minutes. Just long enough for Mary to wonder if he would come back at all. Long enough for her to drag the first reindeer up the rickety ladder by all herself and regret her life choices. Who made reindeer so heavy anyway? Oh, that's right.

She was her own worst enemy.

"I think you'll have better luck with this."

David hoisted a massive wooden ladder, nearly double the size of her own. How he managed the behemoth by himself without any magic to speak of, she hadn't the foggiest. Maybe he was part bear.

"Is that a ladder or a tree?" Mary asked, gingerly easing her way down her own plastic ladder and planting her feet on solid ground.

"It was once both of those things, now it is just a ladder," David said.

He had an easy smile and even easier manner. Sometimes Mary didn't see him for weeks on end when he worked the night shift as a paramedic. When he did, the neighborhood kids came in turns to walk Pirate and play with her in the yard. Lately, he'd had a nearly human schedule with reasonable on and off hours. Mary found she appreciated seeing him around more.

"So, what's the plan?" he asked.

"The plan is to make them fly," Mary said, hands on hips as she glared at the reindeer she'd created. She may have been overenthusiastic in her plan, but it was what she wanted. She would have flying reindeer. Magic or not.

David looked at the reindeer and then at the roof. The single reindeer she had dragged up had tipped over and was dangling from the edge. David glanced at Mary again, as if confirming her insane plan to make the life-sized

Santa and reindeer—and an actual full-sized sleigh—fly. He chuckled quietly to himself.

"I'll be right back," David said, securing the mighty ladder against her house. "Don't use that without me." And then he walked back to his home, digging into his pockets for his phone.

While he was away, Mary secured the red harnesses around the mannequin deer, the silver bells tinkling at every move. David promised he would return, and so he would.

Apparently, with reinforcements.

David had called some of his friends over from the hospital. Mary recognized the paramedics and firefighters David had begun to call friends. It was a new line of work for the man. She was happy he had found solace with his daughter living so far away. Even more happy when those burly young men started discussing how best to achieve her goal.

"You want those… up there?" one of them asked, incredulous.

"Yep," Mary confirmed. "I did it last year, and it was a huge success."

"And you didn't break your neck?" It was David's paramedic friend.

Mary wasn't about to tell him that last year she could do

whatever she wanted because she was a living breathing fairy tale creature. One who had the power to cover mountains in snow and paint houses with starlight. Magic in her blood begged to be used, but a bargain was a bargain. This year, she truly was the feeble old lady who lived next door without any help or family to speak of.

She hated it.

"Well, it seemed a lot smaller last year," Mary said.

"Well then, I guess we'll get 'em up there," the firefighter was saying. "I've never been afraid of any ladders."

And that was that.

The group of them came up with a plan to make reindeer fly, mainly fishing wire and industrial super glue David had in his garage. The sleigh was a smidgen more complicated. The men would absolutely not hear of her angling it over the edge of her roof the way she had last year. There were too many emergency personnel among them to let that structural hazard stand. But with some two-by-fours, some roofing nails, a little tar, and a cleverly hidden security rope, they managed to get the sleigh secured for take-off.

Santa, after all the rest, was the easiest part. Once the reindeer were flying and the sleigh was soaring, all Santa had to do was kick back and enjoy the ride. The irony was not lost on Mary.

She thanked her crew with hot chocolate and cookies before sending them all home. Normal, everyday, absolutely *not* magical cookies.

CHAPTER EIGHTEEN

Blackout

When dawn broke on the morning of Thanksgiving, the air was crisp, the wind biting. There was a sliver of blue daylight gently unspooling into gold as the sun began to crest the horizon. The holiday would soon settle over all of them. Neighbors would prepare for welcoming loved ones.

Then, the magic would really begin.

Mary Christmas stood in the road, contemplating the overall effect of her latest addition to her Victorian craftsman home. She had spent the greater part of the previous evening molding giant spheres of ice into globes of light. The first attempt had resulted in nothing more than a muddy puddle and a frustrating encounter with the neighbors. Mary knew she would have to abandon the no-magic rule just this once and spun the shimmering spheres of ice herself.

The new snow globes were coated in her personal permafrost that would protect them from melting and keep their sugary dusted exterior throughout the season.

"Yoo-hoo! I see you've added snow globes!" a snooty voice called from across the street. "Well, so have I!" Phyrne declared.

Mary turned to find Phyrne in her thin silk bed robes. How the woman managed to be this ridiculous before the sun was even up… The quiet hum of morning was broken by the whirring of Phyrne's motors spinning to life. The deflated blobs Mary had overlooked previously slowly filled with air. The polyvinyl unfolded into shapely forms of polar bears, snow globes, and caroling angels. It was a simple addition, if a little unimaginative, that complimented the pearl sheen of iridescent lights covering the woman's home.

She had to begrudgingly admit Robin had done an excellent job crafting a winter wonderland of light for Phyrne. And he wasn't alone. Up and down the street, motors whirred with life, neighbors leaving them on to greet the day rather than waiting for dusk. Every house, it seemed, was finally ready to celebrate.

Phyrne smugly turned her back on Mary, sauntering in

her front door. Mary growled under her breath. Their decorations could not be more opposite. Phyrne had gone for geometry and swatches of colorless lights. Mary had turned her home into a bonafide gingerbread house. She would not be surprised if Baba Yaga came for a visit to test her oven.

Mary made her way inside as the first round of sedans and minivans began to arrive. They lined the streets and filed neatly into driveways. Families were coming together to help finish stuffing turkeys or roasting vegetables. Mary Christmas had no such plans, though she was pleased to have Mr. Crabtree coming. And Robin, if he got over himself.

She had prepared everything last night rather than rush around like a chicken without feathers trying to cross the road today. She had completed all her preparation from peeling and boiling potatoes to cutting green beans and frying onions. She'd even made her mother's creamy mushroom soup from scratch before seasoning the turkey and leaving it to marinate all night. All she would have to do today was stuff the bird, set the oven to the right temperature, and enjoy a hot toddy while she waited.

She arranged her turkey in a roasting pan with a large ceramic cup filled with cider. She was quite fond of the black and bronze antique triple oven stove. Even in the harshest of winters, she could always warm a cup of tea or bake her cookies because all she needed was a little fire in the bottom pan if the modern amenities failed her. She set the turkey inside and latched the door with a firm click.

It occurred to her as she set her turkey timer that she had not yet made her cookies. And of course she was going to need lots of cookies this season if all her work was to be complete. She set her second oven to temperature as she gathered her butter, sugar, and flour. It took her some time to find the nutmeg, again, tucked behind a jar of peanut butter of all things. Just a dash of the nutty spice was enough to enrich her famous shortbread cookies. She scooped, leveled, cut, and kneaded her dough until it was just right.

The second oven dinged to alert her the interior had reached its desired temperature, just as she finished setting her chilled dough on the marbled counter. She dusted it with a pinch more flour and fine powdered sugar before she began rolling out the dough into a thin sheet.

She had a multitude of cookie shapes, and she often used whatever came to her hand first. But today, it had to be snowflakes. She cut each cookie with care, lifting them from their stencil with a flat spatula and resting them on the waiting pan. When she was finished, she rolled the remaining bits into small balls and pressed them flat with a spoon before dropping a dollop of strawberry jam on each.

She was just about to set them in the oven when her entire house went dark. The electricity escaping the veins of the house was like the sound of a mountain troll swallowing a lamb. She set the sheet of unbaked cookies back on the counter, checking around the house for any sign of pulsing life in the coppery entrails. But even the shadow box in the subbasement sat undisturbed. Not a single breaker was switched to red waiting for a reset. Nothing was tripped or broken.

The electricity was simply gone.

Mary tugged on her favorite green princess coat and winter boots to step outside. She may have been overzealous with her winter wind last night when she had cured her ice globes. She wanted to see if perhaps in her haste she had felled a tree, but what greeted her surprised her.

The entire street was dark with an abnormal quiet. Neighbors from up and down the block were beginning to exit their homes in search of a source. They looked from face to face, congregating in the center where Mary, Robin, and Phyrne's houses faced off. They were by far the most aggressive with their decorations to date. And many of the faces were unhappy with them.

"This is your fault!" Phyrne snapped. She was the most

disheveled Mary had ever seen her. Half her hair was in fat turquoise curlers, the rest limply hanging around her ears. Her make up contouring was unblended, making her look like a rabid urban tiger. And she had wrapped herself in her husbands warm robe again.

"You think so?" Mary said, her eyebrows raised in disbelief. She wasn't the one with a million strands of lights on every square inch of her roof. She only had twelve. Of course they were each 200 feet long, but who was keeping track anyway?

"Yes!" Phyrne barked. "You ruined Thanksgiving for all of us!"

"If fault belongs to anyone, it's you Mrs. Nesbitt." Selena, among others had started to gravitate toward the noise of the fight. Her hair was up in a loose messy bun, she wore boots and her college sweats as if she wasn't quite prepared for people at this hour. Magdelena was on her hip still in her pajamas. It occurred to Mary perhaps Selena was so deep in her preparation for cooking the holiday meal she hadn't had time to dress herself, or anyone else in the Ortiz household.

"My fault?" Phyrne was affronted.

"You better believe it," Bethany Montgomery said. She was a formidable woman in her mid-fifties, living alone for nearly ten years since her husband had passed. She made every holiday meal for her two grown nephews and sister now.

Phyrne sputtered. "But we always—"

"The whole block is dark." Sandra and her daughter had made it to the front of the growing crowd. They had the same harried air of panic as they prepared Thanksgiving for their small family. "Maybe more. It's hard to tell how far it goes."

"Our entire neighborhood is without power because of you!" Bethany said.

"She's right. This *is* your fault!" Someone called from the back.

"I did no such thing!" Phyrne shouted back. More and more neighbors had joined the ever growing congregation of curious onlookers.

"It was your idea to pressure the entire neighborhood into a decoration stand off," Bethany said firmly, hands planted on her hips. Her hair was wrapped in a purple top-knot scarf and she wore comfortable matching sweats. "You made dang sure this whole neighborhood danced to your tune and pulled out all their decorations." She glared at Phyrne and then directed her attention to Mary with a lifted eyebrow.

Bethany had never gotten on well with Phyrne, but Mary was unused to being on the receiving end of her anger. It left her feeling strange. She looked about. Bethany wasn't alone.

The whole block was indeed dark, not a single wisp of light through any window. Any decorations that required electricity were somber, the drooping corpses of inflatables flat and lifeless against the ground.

"Both of you! Your stupid feud is going to ruin Thanksgiving for everyone," another neighbor cried.

"It's not my fault!" Phyrne wailed defensively.

"Yes, it is," Mary admitted quietly. Every head swiveled to look at her. Phyrne shot a vengeful glare at Mary, which Mary chose to ignore. From a look down the block, the black out went much further than their quiet little street. It seemed the entire neighborhood might very well be without power.

"You and I, both. We did this. We've been so hung up making the other miserable we neglected to notice how our efforts might affect our friends."

"I am not your friend!" Phyrne snapped. "And I refuse to take responsibility for any of this. I'm without power too. I can't restore it. I'm not a witch! Ask *her!*"

No amount of magic could make the electricity come back on. Her powers were elemental, but lightning and electricity were not the same thing even if they shared similar energy. Mary could not restore the power grid, though she would very much like to.

"Very well, Phyrne. No one's blaming you. At least, not only you," Mary said. Phyrne sucked in a breath of protest, but Mary pressed on. "But we can make it right."

Her voice carried, and she found herself at the center of the community. There were few friendly faces. This season had been an unrelenting skirmish between adults as if they were schoolyard children. Mary quite enjoyed a petty rivalry, but not at the expense of innocent bystanders, like Selena and her children. Not at the expense of people like Bethany or Mr. Crabtree. Or Jade and her mother.

"How?" a deep voice demanded. Miles Henry was a tall man with a no nonsense air about him. His haircut and rigid posture suggested time in the armed forces. He was surrounded by a gaggle of children and relatives and looked ready to plow through anything that got in the way of his family's celebration. "How do you think you can save Thanksgiving, Miss Christmas?"

Mary didn't have any particular feelings—good or bad—for Thanksgiving. It wasn't her holiday. Like most holidays, she found people adored it or despised it. She just enjoyed the food. It was abundantly clear from her neighbors' faces, however, that they most certainly had strong feelings about the day. Their faces were somber and tight with anxiety.

Well, she was Queen, wasn't she? Not that any of the neighbors knew that. She could do *something* to at the very least fix their day.

"Does anyone have any experience with cooking over open fires?" Mary asked in a dubious tone. There were general murmurs, but no one stepped forward. "Oh, come now. I can not be the only one who has ever cooked in a cauldron."

"No one else is a witch," someone grumbled from beyond Mary's sight. Her eyes narrowed as she searched for the speaker, but when no one stepped forward she chose to move on. For now.

"Alright. Ladies and gentleman, we can save Thanksgiving *if* we work together. We need firewood, coal barbecues, and as many cast iron pans as you can spare. Ceramic or even stainless steel will do, but heaven help you if you bring me any teflon toxic nonsense," Mary ordered.

"For those of you who don't wish to participate in food preparation, perhaps you can gather blankets and gloves so no one loses any fingers or toes."

Mary would send a gentle urge to the autumn winds to stay clear of the street while they worked. Maybe hold off entirely until tomorrow, just in case.

"Well, let's get moving, people. These fires won't build themselves. Chop, chop!" Mary clapped her hands in rapid succession.

The authority in her voice sent grousing neighbors back to their homes. She worried no one would return, but within minutes, her favorite neighbor, David Bly, had wheeled an entire cord of wood to the foot of Mary's driveway.

"I figure you have the cauldron, so you could use the wood," he said it with a wink. "I'll bring back my barbecue in a minute. Think I may run to the store to get more coals if I can find one open. If we're going to wood-fire this meal for a city block, we're gonna need more than what I have in my garage."

"Thank you, David." She nodded regally towards him as he unloaded the wood into a pile.

He gave her a merry smile, beaming through his well trimmed beard. There was a bittersweet look in his eyes, the sorrow at the loss of his wife and absence of his adult daughter readable in the creases around his weathered face. Mary would have to do something about that girl. Tomorrow. David's daughter could be tomorrow's problem. For now, she was grateful he was here.

"Need help building a fire?" Robin asked.

Mary shot him a look. "If you can't see what needs

doing without instruction then what use do I have for you?"

She knew she was being unfair. Robin didn't seem to notice. He just set about arranging the wood in a more accessible pile near Mary's giant cauldron. Maybe it was serendipitous that she had been petty this year and still had it out where she could make some use of it.

She dismantled the stuffed witches' hats and globes of glass from the interior bell of her cauldron. The baubles she had cemented onto the exterior with clay were more stubborn as if reluctant to let go. A press of her finger to the side of her nose with a whisper of words and they tumbled neatly into her grass.

"What do I do with this?" Selena asked.

She had shifted into a reasonable purple Columbia parka stuffed with feathers and blue jeans. Behind her, she pulled a Radio Flyer wagon loaded with several cast-iron pots and Dutch ovens trailing behind her.

Mary smiled.

CHAPTER NINETEEN

It Takes a Village

Over the course of the next several hours, Mary directed neighbors into circling their barbecues in the road and setting the coals to blazing. David made several trips to the store and returned with charcoal enough for everyone and an extra tankard of propane for Miles's behemoth of a double grill.

Robin built fires nearby in portable pits, arranging them in a protective circle to keep as much heat centered in the ring as possible. He stoked each fire from a pile of wood that kept replenishing itself no matter how much everyone burned. Mary only shot him a suspicious look once. He blinked at her innocently. She snorted and whispered to the wind to pull the smoke away from the center without stealing the warmth they had built.

Several of the community mothers and grandmothers started an assembly line of plastic folding tables where food was prepared. Root vegetables were chopped and piled into ceramic Dutch ovens before being centered on coal fired racks. Some brilliant soul had prepared enough colcannon potatoes to feed an army the night before in their twenty-two quart ceramic slow cooker. The earthenware vat had been hefted into a barbecue to gently start warming.

The air took on a savory aroma of sage, rosemary, and thyme floating over a buttery, smoked scent of roasting foods. The largest turkey Mary had ever seen, courtesy of Miles Henry, was stuffed with butter and herbs, then hoisted into her own cauldron. Several smaller turkeys were added to the giant roasting pan, painted in the same butter and seasonings to compliment Miles' contribution.

A wire rack frame bolstered the roasting pan above the base so the hot air could circulate around the pan like a real oven. Sticks of butter and a ceramic mug brimming with apple cider from Robin Goodfellow's personal brew bubbled in a steel pot under the roasting pan.

It had taken three adult men to lift the cauldron lid and close the turkey in for roasting. Mary just smiled politely and batted her lashes at them when they marveled at how the heck she had got the damn thing in the the yard in the first place.

The blackout was slowly morphing into a community block party. Mary couldn't have orchestrated it better if it had been intentionally planned. She paused every so often to appreciate the sights and sounds. Children playing an epic game of tag, secure in the safety of the street because their parents had parked cars at each end to block unexpected traffic. Someone had brought out a guitar and others joined as they circled around a fire and began to sing folk songs and Christmas carols. It was a magical surreal scene. Mary thought she might capture and recreate the moment in one of her globes.

"Cider?" Robin asked.

He hovered just behind her, two mugs in his calloused palms. She smiled approval and nodded, accepting the delectable brew with gratitude. She inhaled the aromas rich with currants, orange, and cloves.

The scent flooded Mary with a barrage of pleasing memories from her early childhood many, many moons ago. There had been warm community fires just like this. Mothers fussed over large iron pots and pans, everyone specializing in an old family recipe made to share. No one ate alone. Every meal was a community event. Every meal was about family.

"This is how it should always be," Mary said dreamily as she sipped her cider and sighed, eyes brimming with the memories.

"Dark and ominous?" Robin asked.

Mary shot him an irritated look. "Friends and family coming together. Taking care of one another. It's what this holiday was *supposed* to be. For better and worse."

"For better and worse?"

"Not everyone has a healthy relationship with their family," Mary said.

She herself had wanted a different life so badly she had abandoned everything she knew and loved. It was how she had become the Winter Queen. But that was a tale for a different night. Tonight, she looked around at her found family, her found community, and basked in the glow of their joy.

"Ma'am?" A gentleman in neon yellow and orange winter clothes and an official looking hard hat approached Mary and Robin with caution. From the look of him, he was from the electric company attempting to source the blackout and fix the problem.

"What can I do for you, Mr. Lineman?" Mary asked.

"Abel, ma'am. Ian Abel. I'm here investigating the blackout. I asked the neighbors, and they said you were in charge." Robin snorted, and Mary amicably stomped on his foot to shut him up.

"In charge is a loose term," Mary said smoothly. "Though I am helping organize our community meal so that no one goes hungry on this prodigious day."

"Yes, well…" Ian looked from Mary to the two households, both alike in gluttonous decorations. Phyrne and Mary, even in their darkened hallow, were clearly the most exuberant in expressing their enthusiasm for the upcoming holidays.

"Best I can figure is these two houses exceeded their power limitations for the grid. Maybe when all the houses together turned on the switch for dinner and the lights… Well, best I can tell the pull of power was just too much for the grid."

"Understandable." Mary nodded in agreement. She wasn't in the least bit surprised. "What can be done to remedy the situation?"

"I… well, we're working on getting it back on line as quickly as we can. But in the event that we do turn back on all your lights, well, I'm sorry to say it may just have to be a little less festive this year."

Mary slowly turned her entire attention to the young man. He was in his late twenties with lean muscles and a sharp jawline. His hair was dusty blonde and his eyes the warm brown of a sequoia tree.

"Are you telling me," Mary slowly began her approach, like a cat preparing to pounce, "that with all of our modern technology, with all of our modern infrastructure, with all the gods forsaken *BILLS* we pay through the nose every time a cloud rolls by that we can not have our Christmas decorations to our liking? Is that what you're telling me, Mr. Ian Lineman Abel?"

Ian swallowed under Mary's scrutiny, his Adam's apple bobbing uncomfortably under his skin. Just out of her peripheral, Mary saw Robin step forward, sliding a familiar arm over the young man's shoulder.

"It's not you, Ian. I don't think your bosses understand just how seriously this neighborhood takes Christmas," Robin soothed the man, a flick of twinkling eyes aimed at Mary. She scowled.

"Yes, but—"

"Yes, but nothing," Robin interrupted. "These two houses are just the beginning. They may be the flagships, the pinnacle anchors of the block, but the rest of these neighbors, they're just getting started. Come Christmas the whole block is gonna be lit up like the Vegas strip. There will be an awful lot of children in this city who will be disappointed if they can't see Mary Christmas's house in all its splendor. You wouldn't want to disappoint the children, would you, Ian?"

"You're Mary Christmas?" Ian asked.

Mary crossed her arms, resuming her aloof indifference. She was caught somewhere between the matronly grandmother who baked cookies and the vicious crone who set black ice under your tires just to watch you spin.

Something shifted in the young man's face as he looked at her. As if he saw past the villain she pretended to be and only saw Mrs. Claus.

"Okay, We'll see what we can do," Ian said.

"See that you do," Mary purred.

The children found Mary a moment later, a breath of time when she wasn't directing anyone and had nothing to do with herself. They invited her to play a game and dragged her to where their father had set up some boards with holes in them. The Ortiz children called the game corn hole and had been attempting to explain the point of this game to Mary for some time.

Mary was so confused. "So, I just… throw this bag of rice—"

"Bean bag," Jax corrected her.

"And I just—"

"Throw it at the board over there," Carlos instructed.

"And then what happens?"

"Then, you win!" Magdelena shouted.

"*Cállate*," Jax said. "If you make it in the hole, you earn points. If you miss you don't get any points."

"I see. And the point of this game is…"

"You have fun," a rich baritone voice joined the chorus.

Mary looked up to see Robin watching them. He was dressed warmly in layers of flannel, blue jeans, and heavy black boots. He wore his reversible coat that was red velvet on one side and black fur on the other. It hid well what the coat really was—his Santa coat.

"When was the last time you had fun?" Mary taunted.

"I rather enjoyed our impromptu concert of silver bells," Robin said mildly.

The children's attention ping-ponged back and forth from Mary to Robin. She could tell that at least the older ones were still dubious either of them were the magic gift makers of Christmas. At least Magdelena had accepted it as fact with no evidence to the contrary. Mary was Mrs. Claus, Robin was Santa. He got the better end of that faith as far as Mary was concerned.

"Yes, well. Let's give it a whirl," Mary said.

Mary brought her arm back, bean bag in hand. She aimed for the board about five paces away from her and tossed the bag under hand. It arched through the air in an inverted crescent before it thunked against the wood with a firm thwack and dropped through the hole.

"You did it!" The children whooped and hollered in celebration.

"I did it!" Mary clapped her hands, delighted.

"You did it! You did it! You did it!" Magdelena shouted again, throwing both arms around Mary's legs in a bearish squeeze that Mary supposed was a hug.

"Oh, why thank you," Mary said, patting the girl on the goofy pink pom of her winter hat. Mary felt a strange surge of joy. Perhaps that was the point of the game. Not to win, or lose, but to enjoy. Have fun, as Robin had told her to do.

"Nicely done," Robin said. He uncrossed his arms and approached the boards with intention. He bowed slightly at his hips, hand extended in quiet request. "May I?"

Jax plopped a bag into his hand before Mary could think to tell him no. In the next breath, Robin was aiming, his focus intent on his task. Mary was having none of it. She whispered to the wind and felt it respond in kind, streaking through the street at the precise moment Robin's bag would have dropped effortlessly through the hole. He glowered at Mary as his bag thunked and stuck to the wooden board.

"Bad luck, my friend," Mary said.

Robin's lips thinned into a line. "I think I'll go restock the firewood."

"He won't take away Christmas, will he Mrs. Claus?" Magdelena asked quietly.

"What?" Mary was startled by the question.

"Because he lost the game," Jax explained. "She thinks he won't come for Christmas if he's mad."

"Goodness me, he better not," Mary said. Seeing Magdelena's distraught face, she took pity on the girl. She knelt to look Magdelena in the eye.

"You listen to me, Magdelena Ortiz. Nothing will keep Christmas from your door this year. I promise." Relief washed over the girls face and her smile returned. "Now, go find you mama and see if she needs any help. All of you. Dinner is just about ready."

Savory smells indeed permeated the air. Children who had drifted away from the warmth of the fires to play games now floated back to their mothers. Quick hands tried to snatch freshly baked rolls only to be thwarted by their aunties with a quick rap on the knuckles. The musicians began to pack up and exchange their equipment for plates and serving utensils. Side dishes made their way to folding tables hastily converted into a buffet line.

Grandparents wrangled children into the line while the host of each barbecue and fire pit served directly onto people's plates as they passed by. An epicurean worth of mismatched lawn chairs had been arranged in the eye of the circle warmed by fires as people began to eat. Everyone settled into the low murmur of chewing and quiet conversations.

Mary found her own way around to each station, spooning turkey, green beans, and stuffing onto her plate. She was about to snag a dollop of the colcannon potatoes onto the side of her plate when she spotted Cyrus hefting a large cast iron Dutch oven out of his own barbecue with thick kitchen mitts. She wandered over.

"Good evening, Mr. Crabtree," Mary said.

"When you invited me to dinner, I did not expect we would enjoy the company of the entire neighborhood," Cyrus said, a smile in his warm brown eyes. His signature braids fell over a warm wool jacket he'd paired with heavy blue jeans.

"Neither did I," Mary said with a laugh.

"It is good for our community, this shared meal. I think we were all beginning to forget ourselves with bitterness and petty rivalries," Cyrus said, as he settled the hot Dutch oven on a thick serving pad and raised a knowing eyebrow at Mary.

"Yes, well. In spite of our best efforts, the universe has conspired to bring us all together," Mary hummed in agreement. "What is that positively sinfully delightful smell?"

Cyrus smiled and removed the top of his Dutch oven. A wave of steam carried the scent of garlic, butter, and rosemary to her. She inhaled deeply and sighed.

"My mother's recipe," Cyrus said. "Rosemary thyme biscuits. They satisfy the soul and cleanse the spirit."

"Do they really?" Mary asked, intrigued as she floated closer to take another whiff.

"I have no idea," Cyrus said, a twinkle in his eyes. "It's just what my mother always said. Would you like a biscuit?"

"Maybe just one. With a little butter… And honey?"

Cyrus laughed. "That is the only way to enjoy a biscuit."

He served Mary, cutting the biscuit and slathering it with butter and honey. She couldn't help herself. She had to take a bite right then and there.

"Oh, my. Cyrus, these might be the best biscuits I've ever had," Mary gushed, stuffing the remaining bits in her mouth.

"One more?" He asked, his brown skin crinkled as he smiled.

Mary nodded and waited patiently as he prepared her a second serving. Cyrus grinned.

"Mary Christmas!" The littlest Ortiz darted though the crowd and crashed into Mary's legs, nearly knocking Mary to the ground. "I saved you a spot!"

Mary looked back to Cyrus, expectantly. She felt a twinge of guilt not fulfilling their dinner plans. Even more that she had forgotten about them in the rush to get everything arranged.

Cyrus Crabtree was a good man, with a kind and gentle heart. He smiled at her warmly, waving her on as he helped the next person in line. "Go. We can not keep children waiting. I'll see you later."

"Thank you, Cyrus. Perhaps we can raincheck our dinner for another night? I've always wanted to learn that card game you always play, what's it called?"

"Solitaire is not a great game for two, but perhaps we can play something else. Gin Rummy would be nice," he said.

"I'm quite fond of gin, I didn't know it was a card game."

Cyrus laughed. "Yes, well. Raincheck it is. Enjoy your biscuit."

The cherub cheeked Magdelena tugged on Mary's green jacket sleeve. She followed the girl to a pack of coolers being used as benches where the Ortiz family had assembled.

"I invited Mrs. Claus to join us!" Magdelena proudly declared. "Hey! That's my seat!" She pouted, shooing her older brother Jax off of a small cooler she had saved.

"Mrs. Claus?" her father Mateo asked, the corner of his eyes crinkled in amusement.

"Yes," Magdelena said hotly. "Didn't Mama tell you? So, you better be good, or you won't get any presents this year."

Magdelena's mother flushed, a sheepish smile on her full lips. She shrugged and tilted her head toward her youngest. She must have reaffirmed to her children Mary Christmas was in fact *the* Mrs. Claus to get them to behave. Mary laughed, claiming the seat the little defender of Christmas had provided.

"Mama made churros! You must try one!" Magdelena scampered off to the buffet table before anyone could say anything.

"You made churros? In this chaos?" Mary asked. She was impressed in spite of herself.

"Magic," Selena teased, a wave of her fingers in the air. Mary blinked in surprise, a forkful of green beans halfway to her mouth.

"I made them yesterday," Selena laughed. "We reheated them in foil beside the pumpkin pie. They're nearly as good as they would have been fresh."

"Nearly," her husband said through a mouthful of turkey. Selena playfully smacked his shoulder with the back of her hand.

"I got one!" Magdelena called triumphantly. She had returned with a confection coated in sugar and spices wrapped in wax paper.

"Thank you, my dear girl!" Mary said.

Forget dinner, Mary was having baked goods first. She sighed in pleasure as the sugar and spice dissolved over her tongue. It was nearly as magical as her own cookies.

Nearly.

A muffled electronic beep chirped loudly. The melody reminded Mary of jingle bells as it trilled. Selena checked her watch and sighed in apprehension.

"Mary?" Selena asked, as she set down her finished plate of food. "I was wondering if you could help me check the pie? I've never cooked one in a cast iron before. Reheating churros is one thing, but pie from scratch…"

"Duty calls," Mary said, gently setting Magdelena back on the ground and balancing her mostly full plate out of the way lest she spill on the energetic youngling.

Selena had set up for cooking in a portable fire pit under Mary's careful watch early in the evening. They had leveled the monstrous iron pit at the foot of her driveway, leaving plenty of room for safety. It had been a similar process to how Mary's own mother educated her on open flame cooking all those moons ago. It brought a bittersweet pang of longing and loss to her heart.

Selena opened the cast iron lid with the fire tongs while Mary checked the crust for consistency and color. It looked just about right. Now it needed to be pulled from the flame before the fire could burn it.

"It's perfect," Mary said.

"So, how do I get it out?" Selena asked. Mary smiled, using the hook and pulling the big pan away from open flames. She handed Selena a pair of mighty thick wool gloves to pull the pie pan from the wire rack above the fire. She set the pie to rest on a chunk of log cut and set on its end like a side table.

"Now what?"

"Well, if you want to eat it hot, it will be set enough in five minutes," Mary said. "If you want it cool, you'll need to wait longer."

"I don't think I've ever had a hot pumpkin pie," Selena said, confusion creasing her brows.

"It's much the same, just warmer. You can dollop ice cream or whip cream and treat it like any other hot pie."

Selena nodded. "Thank you, Mary."

"Happy to help! Now, if you'll excuse me. I think I'll finish my beans before they get cold."

Mary gathered her plate and returned to her own gate where she leaned between Jack and Sally. The pair still wore their Christmas stocking caps and lopsided toothy gargoyle grins, along with the rest of the stone faced brood. The hats had made it through the month. Between one bite and the next she decided the gargoyles would be staying for the foreseeable future. Possibly forever.

She grinned and scooped more beans into her mouth.

"Well, what do you have to say for yourself?" Phyrne demanded.

She had given up on her hair and thrown in back in a ponytail. But the tiger stripes had at least been blended enough she wasn't scaring small children. She had wrapped her body in several layers of an obnoxiously bright yellow coat, gloves, hat, and scarf. Not to mention winter boots and snow pants.

Mary didn't understand all the fuss. It was just a light autumn evening. It wouldn't even get chilled enough for a frost. Mary had made sure of it.

"I have no idea what you mean," Mary replied flatly through a mouthful of green beans.

"You ruined Thanksgiving!"

"Did I?" Mary asked. "Look around you, does Thanksgiving look as though it is *ruined*?"

Phyrne made a show of scanning the street with disdain. Mary followed her gaze, making sure to memorize every detail. The children who had already gone back to playing tag. The grandparents huddled near fires with blankets on their laps and hot beverages in their hands. They laughed merrily with one another.

Invited friends and guests floated in and out of the small groups, searching for familiar faces. Mothers and father's told the tale of the black out for the late arrivals and how this Friendsgiving came to be.

The wandering guitarist eventually settled in the middle of like minded musicians and began to strum Christmas carols. As the confidence of the musicians grew, so did the strength of their voices. Neighbors drifted toward them as if called, adding their voices to the harmony when they knew the song, listening in contentment when they didn't.

"Well?" Phyrne snarked.

"Phyrne, if you can't see it, then I can't help you," Mary said.

Phyrne stomped her foot in protest, and Mary just watched her for a long moment. Phyrne, realizing she wasn't about to goad Mary into a fight, stormed away toward her home.

Mary nodded to a passing pair of parents who nodded back with a smile. She raised a forkful of potatoes in salute and began to gleefully eat her food before it truly did get cold. She closed her lips around a mouthful of green beans and sighed. In all, it had been a pleasing evening. It had been a lot of hard work, but she was thankful to find that when it mattered, the community she had chosen to set her roots down in had come together.

CHAPTER TWENTY

Bright Lights

Honestly, Mary was really quite surprised it had taken Phyrne this long to call for the police.

There were just some people who could not handle things on their own, always involving the "authorities," always asking to see the manager. This was just who Phyrne was.

Mary took great delight in ruining the woman's day.

"So, as you can see… we had to check. Two calls in one week on the same household," the taller of the two men was also the older, more seasoned officer. The name badge read Bauer. He was nonplussed at being summoned to check on Mary Christmas over her… well, he wasn't exactly sure what the complaint was this time. His opinion was all over his face, plain as day.

"Quite right, Officer," Mary soothed. "You absolutely must investigate and uncover." Uncover what, Mary hadn't the foggiest.

"Right, well. We just wanted to apologize. We can see you are complying with community standards and nothing seems to be out of the ordinary," Officer Bauer said. His eyes kept shifting back towards the bonfires and charcoal barbecues up and down the street.

"Sarge, I don't remember anything about a community block party on Thanksgiving," the younger officer said. "Is that maybe what this is all about?"

Mary had no doubt it was. One last attempt by Mrs. Nesbitt to make this whole debacle Mary's fault alone.

"Why yes, officers. You see, the power grid has failed us I'm afraid. Too much oomph in our decorations. We do take the holidays so seriously around here," Mary went on and on as if it was perfectly normal.

"I see that." Officer Bauer looked around at the neighborhood decorations, lilting and devoid of light. Each house just as dark. And yet, dozens of small fires and individual barbecues up and down the street. A block party for the ages, if only the decorations had electricity.

"Of course, we simply couldn't let the little ones go without a Thanksgiving," Mary continued blithely. She could see the connections connecting in Officer Bauer's mind. They may have come together as a community, but it was a decidedly grey area for legality with the fires and barbecues in the street. Mary hated rules.

"You see, all the mothers have worked so hard preparing their feasts. It would have been a rotten shame for it all to go to waste. Thank goodness we have some clever outdoorsy types who helped us get those birds roasting over charcoals and those pies baking in fires."

"You cooked Thanksgiving turkey over open fires?" The younger of the two officers was thunderstruck. Officer Bauer was grinning from ear to ear, a glazed hungry look as he took in all the food and community.

"Have you gentlemen had dinner yet? There is plenty to go around," Mary invited them.

"Oh, well, we couldn't. We're on duty," the younger of the two said.

"Jimmy? Is that you?" David Bly with his impeccable timing clapped both officers on the shoulder. "What are you boys doing in this neck of the woods?"

"Got a call about illegal… well, fires, I suppose," Officer Jimmy Bauer explained.

"Nothing illegal about a neighborhood coming together on a holiday. Especially with the lights all out. Whole block has been dark all day," David said. "Besides, Jason and

Ash just got off shift and are here, too. We're all having a good time."

David gestured to the two firefighters who had helped Mary and David make reindeer fly. They were still in their boots and station clothes, their warm tactical responder parkas stitched with the Maltese Cross on the shoulders. They saluted David and the police officers.

"Hey, Jim! Happy Thanksgiving!" they shouted over their shoulders, as they loaded paper plates with food.

"Come on, have a slice of pie. We made the desserts in the barbecues, too." David beamed at them, ushering the police officers away from Mary.

Phyrne had been watching the encounter from the foot of her driveway, bundled up as tight as a pig in a blanket. Mary thought she looked like one too, come to think of it as Phyrne stomped back to her side of the block at a disgruntled gate. She turned back several times to look at Mary and glare, but she kept going. Thank the stars.

Mary pleasantly sipped her cider. *Final round, knock out,* Mary thought smugly.

As the night wore on, musicians began to congregate closer around fires, strumming guitars or slapping the skin of their drums. One industrious fellow brought out a bassoon. He'd have a fun time keeping that warm enough to stay in tune tonight. Mary silently sent a flick of power his way just so he wouldn't ruin the fun for everyone.

They started out slowly, getting a feel for one another's skills and rhythms. Even as they stuck to more traditional and expected carols, it was still largely improvised. Sometimes they'd forget a chord or rewrite the lyrics on the fly. It wasn't until the singers started to join in that they really caught the spirit of community and blended like a fine wine.

"Nice night," Robin commented, taking up space beside her. He casually leaned against her fence, arms crossed as he surveyed their community like a king. Or a smug rogue who hadn't learned his manners yet. Mary decided she wouldn't seek retribution. Today.

"Everything is as it should be," Mary said.

"I noticed you and Phyrne are back to being sworn enemies," he observed.

Mary snorted.

"Couldn't help but notice how close you two came to being friends before tonight."

Mary felt a twinge of something she couldn't quite define in the pit of her stomach. It wasn't fear or pain. But it was that uncomfortable feeling when truth was about to reveal itself. Truth you already knew, the confirmation as equally disorienting as the not knowing.

"Yes, well. I did try to be friendly. If the little toad wants to continue our rivalry, she'll learn just who she is dealing with," Mary said. There was no venom in it, though, which surprised her. This was her home, her refuge. It would be nice if she didn't always have to play chicken with the neighbors. She sighed ruefully and sipped her cider. It was starting to get cold as the evening temperatures pushed on toward night. She didn't mind. Her belly was full, and her heart was warm enough to last until dawn.

"How's the cider?" Robin asked. His tone was just a little too neutral. His posture a little too casual. Mary tilted her head just enough that she could get a good look at him. His eyes were as bright as stars and his mouth was drawn up into a mischievous smile. He pinched a toothpick between his teeth as he grinned at her.

"What in the all the stars and earth did you put in my cider?"

"Nothing," he said.

Mary relaxed.

"Nothing tonight," he clarified.

"You slimy, deceitful, good for nothing elf!"

"You forgot jolly, merry, and handsome."

"I ought to add you to my gnome collection. Fred could use a companion." Mary was seething.

Robin had the good decency to grimace. "As much as I'd enjoy pissing in your fountain for all eternity…" Robin glanced over his shoulder at the yard.

Mary had decorated her fountain with garlands of fir and ribbons of red. Fred, the little cherub frozen in time with his pants down on the pedestal in the middle, somehow managed to look frigid and uncomfortable in his caricature of a statue.

Robin shuddered. "I think you'd miss me too much."

"Like a toddler misses a bowel movement," Mary snapped.

"Shh, you're attracting their attention."

Several of the neighbors nearest to them had turned their heads toward Robin and Mary. He waved, and Mary saluted her cooling cider mug at them. They waved back and returned to their conversations.

"May I have this dance?" Robin asked, as David's warm baritone, as rich as Johnny Cash, called out in a fierce ballad.

"Excuse me?" Mary was incredulous. She blinked at the boldness, turning her head slowly to appraise him.

Robin had his right calloused hand extended in invitation. His left hand he had tucked behind the small of his back as he dipped in a courtly bow. His merry eyes were hooded by thick lashes as he glanced up. A dimple appeared as his lips turned up in a satisfied grin.

Mary rolled her eyes.

He took the mug from her hand and set it on her gate post beside her beloved gargoyles. "You take care of her cup, Jack. The missus and I are going dancing."

"Oh, for heaven's sake!"

She thumped her hand down into his. Robin slipped a hand into the crook of her bent elbow and gently but firmly led her toward the roaring fires and cluster of musicians. Their voices together were clear and pleasing. A warm baritone paired to a counter alto who harmonized brilliantly. Mary reluctantly allowed herself to be pulled into a lazy waltz.

"You understand there will be consequences?" Mary murmured through smiling teeth.

"I would expect nothing less from you, my queen," Robin agreed. "But what is life without a little consequence?"

She allowed him to lead their dance closer to the fires as he whirled her into a slow boxed waltz, keeping it tight. She could feel the warmth of him through his coat, a light that burned bright within him no matter the season.

More couples joined them, husbands inviting wives, friends embracing each other. Mothers swayed with their toddlers. Jax had boldly invited Jade to dance while Little Magdelena spun in wild circles all on her own with no partner at all. Mary couldn't help herself—she had to smile.

Two of the musicians, Mary noticed as she and Robin swept by, were her favorite neighbors David Bly and Cyrus Crabtree. David played guitar while Cyrus kept tempo with his drum skin. Their voices blended in a rich velvety harmony.

David wore a thick winter coat nearly identical to the one Cyrus wore. Mary wondered how close they were. David's beautiful dog Pirate lay beside him, her gray muzzle nestled on his feet while his fingers picked out chords on his guitar.

Sometime after his daughter left for college and had never returned, he had taken up a litany of hobbies and activities until he found himself in school to be a paramedic. She wondered what he had planned on doing for Thanksgiving before this neighborhood block party. She wondered where he found it in himself with all the heartbreak to sing.

"Pay attention," Robin commanded. "That's twice you've stepped on my toes."

"I'll do a lot more to your toes if it pleases me," Mary growled.

Robin grinned, his eyebrows lifting suggestively.

"That isn't what I meant. You're insufferable!"

Robin laughed and spun her around their circle again.

"How can you not enjoy yourself? Just listen to the music. Look at the stars. When was the last time you danced with friends under the stars?"

Mary quelled him with a look. "I was enjoying myself, but I also noticed our dear friend, David. I want to do something special for him this year."

"Agreed. Maybe bring some joy back to his life. He's been so lost since his daughter left," Robin said.

And then Mary had a wicked idea.

"What would you say if I brought her home for the Christmas?"

"How would you do that?"

"I'm the Queen of Winter, am I not? I can do whatever I wish."

"Last I checked, we were not given power over what's in a person's heart."

"You weren't given power," Mary scoffed, "I, however, can be quite persuasive."

"Is that a fact?"

"It is," she said primly.

"I'll wager that you get in over your head and can't get her home in time for Christmas."

"A bargain? Excellent. What are the terms?"

"You bring his daughter home to his front door by Christmas morning, then for one year and one day I am yours to command," he said.

Mary blinked in surprise. To grant another such power over ones self… Mary Christmas would never wager away her services so freely.

"I get his daughter here for Christmas, and you are mine to do with as I wish?"

"Yes."

Mary considered. She could see no downsides. Yes, it was getting close to the wire here. Thanksgiving would be done in a matter of hours. Christmas was knocking on the door already. Of course, he didn't say it had to be a linear thing. She could use a little magic. Maybe bend the rules of time and see what happened.

Mary smiled. "Deal."

The familiar tingle from her scalp to her toes zipped through her body as the bargain was made. From Robin's toothy grin he was either very confident in the outcome… or he won either way.

Mary scowled at him. "I'm still mad at you about the cider. Bargain or no, you are on my naughty list. There *will* be consequences."

"I wouldn't have it any other way," Robin said, as he turned her out to the length of his arms, tucking her back in tight as he continued. "So, I guess we didn't ruin Thanksgiving."

"The night is young. Give it time," Mary retorted.

"You could just enjoy yourself for a change."

Mary *was* enjoying herself. She looked about and noticed all the neighbors congregating in community. Thanksgiving was a holiday which held a lot of anxiety for a whole lot of people.

Spending time with family when you didn't want to. Not spending time with family when you *did* want to. Then, of course, there were all the people who felt alienated entirely from a holiday for one reason or another. It made it difficult to enjoy for any of them.

It could have gone so badly.

People could have abandoned each other and gone their separate ways. Maybe found an all night diner and ordered a cheeseburger instead. But tonight, for the first time in a long time, people were just people. A tribe of people all living on the same planet. The fates had conspired to bring them all together in this place at this time. And they *had* come together to make the best of a difficult situation.

The musicians eased into a mournful rendition of "I'll be Home for Christmas" as more dancers joined Mary and Robin.

"I am enjoying myself," Mary admitted. "I look around, and I see smiling faces who forgot they were mad at one another and broke bread."

"You know, it was never my intention to start a feud with you. Or with Mrs. Nesbitt for that matter," Robin said.

Mary bristled. "And what was your intention?" She lowered her voice so as not to attract attention or ruin the festive mood that had settled over everyone.

"To see you smile," Robin said.

"I'm sorry?"

"When was the last time you stopped long enough to enjoy a holiday?" Robin asked, spinning Mary around, leading her to the edge away from the circle.

Mary scowled at him. "When was the last time any mother stopped long enough to enjoy any holiday? There would be no holidays without mothers."

"I'm messing this up," Robin sighed, shook his head and tried again. "Mary, what is the purpose of this holiday, of any holiday?"

"To celebrate or honor the subject of the holiday," Mary replied quickly, perturbed by his line of questioning.

"And *this* holiday?"

"This holiday is supposed to be sharing what we have with one another. To say I see you and I honor you," Mary said. It wasn't *her* holiday, but she saw the value in what it should be... What it could be.

"And when has it ever truly been that?"

They had stopped waltzing, instead swaying lazily together as Mary concentrated on what he was saying. Robin was equally invested in how she might reply.

Mary turned her gaze from his and looked around. People were celebrating and honoring each other the way this holiday was intended. Or at least the way Mary had always perceived its intention.

"I may have stoked the fire, provoked you into a feud, hoping this community we have might find it in themselves to come together. I didn't expect it to go this far but..." Robin looked about and smiled. "This is better than anything I could have imagined."

"Me too," Mary had to agree.

As if by divine influence, the electricity for the neighborhood returned at that exact moment. The lights on every house surged into life, showering the dimly lit street in the magic of their glow. Neighbors gasped as they halted conversations and turned their attentions toward their festive homes.

"It's perfect," Mary said.

She wasn't looking at her own home, but at Robin's. The symmetrical patterns he'd crafted, a nebulous of stars winking in perfect harmony over the planes of his home. And in the yard, a glowing wire mesh of a white stag and his queen, watching over a winter fox, a snowy egret, and a Siberian lynx. The creatures of winter, crafted of crystalline starlight. Robin had decorated his home in the winter magic that was Mary Christmas and her realm, her responsibilities.

Her family.

"You're a wretch," Mary accused, wiping away a defiant tear that had escaped her watery eyes.

"I could say the same for you," Robin chuckled.

And she knew it was true. In her final efforts to thwart Phyrne, Mary had morphed from a macabre winter wonderland into a full out gingerbread extravaganza. The scalloped rafters had been coated in a frosting like swath of fabric. When the snows came, it would drape pleasantly and hold the ice where Mary wanted it. The pillars, windows, arches, and every available stretch of plane along her porch had been twined with red ribbons and winking colorful lights, thanks in part to the industrious Ortiz children. Mary had made sure the electrical cords were hidden from view.

In the yard, the large spheres of ice had been shaved to resemble snow globes. Inside each crystal ball was a unique magical dance of winter, also carved of ice. One of Santa taking flight. One of Santa and Mrs. Claus dancing on ice skates, and one of children singing in a choir. The last one had been a particular challenge. Mary was not a bit ashamed to admit she *had* used a touch of magic to etch the details and *keep* them frozen.

She had arranged a toddler sized train that rolled across an invisible track carting wooden toys and elves around the yard. The sleigh Mary had wrestled with was mid take off, the reindeer flying beneath the branches of her tallest tree. They were surrounded by silvery stars of Bethlehem from the craft market. But it was the light of Robin's decorations reflecting off their silvery surfaces and golden bells that made them all glow.

Mary fully expected the crowd to begin to thin now that electricity was back on in their comfortable homes. But they didn't. More chairs were drawn out into the street, and the fires stoked higher. It surprised her.

"Penny for your thoughts?" Robin asked softly. He was watching her, not an ounce of interest in either of their houses.

"I'm marveling at the direction this holiday has taken," Mary said. "And I am pleasantly surprised by it."

"Worth all the petty fighting that led to it?"

Mary narrowed her eyes. "I'll fight tooth and nail against petty dictators with their neighborhood watch badges and flippant grudges." Mary spotted Phyrne chastising one of the Ortiz children for running too fast and knocking into her. Jax barely paused long enough to shout a half hearted apology before he chased after his siblings. They were good kids.

"What do you plan on getting the Ortiz boys for Christmas this year?" Mary asked.

"Jax and Carlos?"

"And Magdelena. She helped me with my cookies. And her mother deserves something special." Selena had been a critical orchestrator in their successful block party. That cast iron pumpkin pie! Mary had never had a better pie.

"What do they want?"

"Aren't you supposed to be omniscient and know these things?" Mary teased.

"Of course, my queen," he replied dryly. "But if they have revealed their heart of hearts to someone they care about…"

Mary smiled. "I know just what to get them."

"And I will be sure to deliver it," he said.

Her smiled widened. They made an excellent team. Robin Goodfellow and Mary Christmas.

"I believe you just might find yourself on the good list this year."

The End

Continue reading for a sneak peek at book two!

CHAPTER ONE

Christmas Cookies

I'd had a hunch flying 3,000 miles home for the holidays was bound to get weird. I just didn't think it would be *this* strange. I didn't think I'd spend my first day back getting into fights with people from my past. I certainly didn't expect to get myself fired in the first twelve hours on the job. But here we are.

So, I sat alone. In a bar. On Christmas… Drowning my sorrows in tequila.

Fantastic.

"Nachos and margaritas at Christmas? Someone is having a tough day." A voice chimed like brass tea bells, somehow beautiful and, at the same time, grating.

"Honestly, nachos are great any time of year," I responded.

"That's very true." I turned to find what I can only describe as a matronly rockstar dressed like Santa's 'little helper' smiling at me. "Mind if I join you?"

Without waiting for an invitation, Mrs. Claus slid down the bar, collecting her rocks glass and cradling it like a lost kitten. I shook my brain, demanding it come back online. I've always been pretty good at noticing my surroundings, but had she been there a minute ago? It felt like she just appeared out of thin air.

How much have I had to drink?

The woman was easily seventy years old, evidenced by her soft powdery cheeks and delicately veined hands. Her intense eyes were the blue of a winter sky just before twilight, glittering with mischief. Perfectly coiffed snow white hair drifted in loose curls down her back. Her surprisingly lithe body was wrapped in a bright red lace over black satin sheath. The garment accentuated her pleasantly firm curves in all the right ways. Even the gaudy gold reindeer belt matched her sleigh-bell earrings.

I have the perfect shoes to go with that belt, my brain mused admiringly. Meanwhile, my nose crinkled in distaste even thinking about my own outfit. I was fashionably challenged in well-loved work boots and soggy snowman socks. All of which complimented my *just-fired* ensemble of black slacks and a buttoned-down white collared shirt. I positively reeked of popcorn and I'd bet good money my red curls had escaped my careful ponytail. I was too afraid to look in a mirror. Little Orphan Annie had gone wild.

It had been *that* kind of day.

"What's a girl like you doing in a place like this?" Mrs. Claus slurred. She'd clearly indulged in generous libations herself before she had started chatting me up. *Aren't we a fine pair of misfits on this Holy Night?*

"Nowhere to go," I admitted mournfully.

A dull ache somewhere between brain freeze and migraine began to thrum at the base of my skull. I ignored it, licking the rim of the bubbled blue margarita glass. Salt and sour mix burst over my tongue. I made the involuntary and unpleasant expression I always make whenever tequila was involved.

"Me neither," Mrs. Claus sighed, smiling warmly as she raised her rocks glass in salute. "It's my one day off a year."

"What made you pick this dive?"

"I spin a globe, point, and go. Here we are," she said with a flourish, settling onto her barstool like a freshly pressed tablecloth. She clutched her beverage to her chest with one hand, offering me her other soft snowy hand. "My name is Mary, Mary Christmas."

"You're serious?" I just managed not to laugh as we shook hands. It was entirely possible I'd had way, *way* too much to drink. "Mary Christmas?"

"That's my name. Don't wear it out." Finding herself terribly amusing, Mary broke into a fit of giggles. Gin and tonic sloshed onto the copper bar top as she tittered.

"You really are Mary Christmas?" I chortled right alongside her.

"At least fifty women named Mary have married a man with the surname of Christmas over the past 170 years," she declared hotly.

"Why would someone know that?" I asked, incredulous.

"Parties. And bars. And because nosy gingerbreads like yourself always ask." She finished her drink and rattled the ice at the bartender. "Another round, if you please, Gerry."

The bartender was already ferrying a plate of nachos to the bar. *Rude!* He'd ordered it before asking me. *Or did I order and forget?* Honestly, I didn't know. But it was nachos. *Who am I to complain?*

"Just tequila this time, please. I don't need any more sugar," I said.

"Oh, tequila! Forget the gin, love. I'll have the tequila, Gerry!" Mary exclaimed excitedly, rapping her knuckles on the bar for emphasis.

Gerry-the-Bartender, a trim, well-groomed gentleman, narrowed his eyes. They were kind eyes, the shade of fresh muddled cider. His face was round and jolly, accustomed to laughter, with deep creases by his eyes and around his mouth. His smile was not intended for us girls. For me and Mary Christmas, he glowered like an ogre, giving us a critical look as he delivered the nachos and collected our used glassware. He suffered a sigh, tilting his head skyward in exasperation as he walked away.

Priorities. Food. I pounced on the nachos, and Mary Christmas joined me. There's comfort in the unabashed confidence of a stranger who had zero issues sharing food she did not order. I munched on a sinful bite of cheese, olives, and tortilla chip before saying: "I'm Zoë by the way."

"Well, of course you are, my girl. Look at you." It was difficult to tell if the British accent was legit or affected. I swallowed more nachos as Gerry-the-Bartender delivered our next round of drinks, shaking his head. Of all the watering holes in all the world, the two of us had to wander into his pub on Christmas Eve. I giggled, blowing my nose with my cocktail napkin.

"Goodness, me. You're a wreck, child!" Mary brushed loose hair out of my eyes with manicured fingers. "What was it, some bloke broke your heart? I can curse him for you if you like."

"What? Oh, no. Thank you. I mean, there was a potential… something. But it didn't work out."

"That's unfortunate."

"It *is* unfortunate. No, I'm upset because I… I was fired tonight."

"Fired?"

"Fired."

"Dashing girl like you? Whatever for?" Mary talked through a mouthful of cheese and toppings. Somehow, it looked delicate and demure on her. I probably looked just this side of feral, wolfing down nachos like a famished goblin.

"Stealing a copy of *Titanic*," I mumbled between bites.

"Oh, I've always wanted to see that film. Is it any good?"

"Um, yeah. I guess." Did Mary live under a rock? Or in some never-never land? I knew I was a bit fuzzy. But how had this woman *not* seen *Titanic*? Hasn't the entire planet? It's on the second… No, third theatrical release?

"Wait, how did you steal a copy of *Titanic*? Is it even in theaters?" she cut off my runaway brain-train and turned toward me with equal parts excitement and confusion.

I shrugged. "It is. I didn't. But a few careless mistakes later… The results speak for themselves."

"Mistakes happen!" Mary cried at the injustice. "I make

them all the time! I just go back and fix them. That's the magic of mistakes. You can fix them."

"God, I wish. I wish this whole day never happened. I wish I could just…" I sighed, dropping my head onto the bar top and wrapping my arms around my throbbing skull.

"Sounds to me like you need a do-over, love," Mary soothed, rubbing my back.

"Yeah, well… that's not a thing. Otherwise, I'd take it," I leaned into her touch, grateful for her kindness and warmth. "What I wouldn't give to go back in time."

"Well, you have had a rough go of it. Here I thought I needed a vacation." Mary Christmas licked the last of the salt off her glass, sucking on the neon straws until she slurped the dregs of sour mix and tequila hiding between the squares of ice. I started laughing uncontrollably, doubling back on my stool until I nearly fell off.

"What in the world could be so funny at this exact moment?"

"Oh, Mary. Mary Christmas. Just… Us." I grinned like an idiot. "Just look at us."

Mary Christmas raked her gaze over me from top to bottom, like a judgey grandmother. She then appraised her own polished holiday attire in the slice of mirrored wall behind the bar before returning her attention back to me.

"Speak for yourself, little gingerbread. I quite like the way *I* look," she replied tartly, smoothing the fabric of her lace dress, then fluffing her snowy hair.

"I mean this," I waved a hand at our empty glasses and the devoured plate of nachos. "Two skirts drinking themselves stupid on Christmas."

"Well, I don't know. I enjoyed the nachos. And the company." She dabbed a gob of beans and salsa away from her signature Chanel red lipstick. With a flick of her wrist, she signaled for Gerry-the-Bartender. "Another round, if you please."

Gerry-the-Bartender approached slowly, exhaling through his nose. He set calloused palms firmly on the bar top, an eyebrow arched at each of us in turn. "I think I'm going to have to call it, ladies."

"What?" I half laughed. I'm the great descendant of a Viking warrior. At least, that's what my untamed mop of curls—which would not have been out of place at a Weasley family reunion—told me. And, at nearly 5'9" with 140 pounds of lean muscle earned through years of disciplined workouts, I was no wilting flower.

A few margaritas are not going to kill me, Gerry. Maybe just make the drinks and don't give me any lip.

I kept those last thoughts to myself.

"Oh, we're calling it, are we?" Mary cooed, cackling at

the absurdity of being cut off at her age. I had to agree. We collapsed into a fit of hysterics. Hot tears streamed down my cheeks, my belly aching. I couldn't remember the last time I laughed so hard. Gerry-the-Bartender shook his head, refilling our waters before abandoning us to our mirth. Mary paused to look at me sideways. Her blue eyes gleamed with a shameless twinkle.

"Fancy a cookie?" she asked quietly.

"A what?" I wiped saltwater from my eyes with the back of my hands. The gesture streaked flaky black eyeliner into geometric patterns on my cheeks. Mary Christmas howled with laughter, amused by my unfortunate Picasso face-scape. Still giggling, she dipped her napkin into water, dabbing at my face as though I were her toddler.

"A cookie, dear. Would you like a cookie?"

"A cookie?" I repeated through hiccuping giggles.

She finished cleaning my face, discarding the crumbling napkin on the bar top. From a green, fur-lined, suede coat pocket she withdrew a box. The lid was embossed with a cartoonish Santa, his sleigh ready to take flight. It glowed when she unclasped the latch, the brass interior refracting the twinkling lights of Christmas. A handful of shortbread cookies lay on a red velvet lining, cut into perfect snowflakes, and dusted with a sprinkle of rock sugar.

"A special cookie," Mary's manicured fingers plucked a single, glittering cookie from the box. "My very own recipe."

"A 'special' cookie?" I chortled. I just bet it was 'special'.

"Magic," Mary whispered. "I promise… You have never had a cookie like this before."

Mary Christmas grinned like a naughty queen of the Keebler elves, popping a cookie into her own mouth. Sublime delight spread across her wintery face, traces of rock sugar clinging to her rouged lips. She licked it off with a swipe of her pink tongue. *Of course, Kris Kringle's crazy ex-girlfriend has a cannabis dispensary in her coat pocket.*

Somewhere, in my tequila-mush-addled brain, I remembered something my mother once told me: *Don't take food from faeries.*

No. That wasn't right. Strangers? Yes, that's the one. Don't take candy from strangers. But Mary Christmas wasn't a stranger. Was she? She cleaned my face with a wet nap. Strangers don't do that.

Oh, why not?

I accepted her offered cookie and popped it into my mouth. The soft buttery confection melted in bursts of home and the pleasant sweetness of Christmas. I had *never* tasted a cookie quite so indulgent. The sensation bordered on magical. My blood warmed, my toes curled, and my fingers tingled.

Maybe it wouldn't be the worst Christmas after all.

CHAPTER TWO

Wake Up, It's Christmas

The ear-shattering obnoxiousness of the Nokia "Jingle Bells" ringtone cut through the morning silence like a katana. Never mind that Nokia was from Finland and the katana was from Japan. It was far too early for this. And who the hell programmed my phone with "Jingle Bells" anyway?

I opened my eyes and immediately regretted my life choices, snapping them shut decisively. A yawn escaped my mouth in a growl I was not entirely sure was English.

Or human.

I ran a hand over my face and racked my brain for clues. It was a strange dream, full of Christmas and sparkling lights.

Even Santa and Mrs. Claus had been there. No, that was the bartender. What bartender? Merry Christmas?

Where am I?

The complex primordial grey matter known as my brain supplied absolutely nothing useful. There was a shrouded fog bank where memory should be. I stretched my stiff muscles to discover myself tucked, rather neatly, under a coffee table. As if someone lovingly and tenderly took the time to make sure no one would step on me.

What. Just. Happened?

My head throbbed with pain and fear. I felt like I was suffocating under the table. I wrapped my fingers around the table legs to pull myself out. A shocking electric pain forced me to retract my hand.

Ow! Was the damned thing made of iron? No, that wasn't right, either. Iron is a terrible conduit for electricity. So, why did I think it was iron?

Well, that's a strange thought first thing in the morning.

"Jingle Bells" trilled again, and I cracked open my eyes. Except for one blinding light nearby, my surroundings were completely dark. A darkness so crushing that the only safe place to stash me would have been under the iron table.

So, why does it feel like a trap?

A thought, somewhere in my mind, reminded me iron

was dangerous. A cage, a prison. Slowly, very slowly, I blinked away the cobwebs of my mind and wiped my mouth with the back of my hand. There was drool on my chin.

The digital beep-beep-beep, beep-beep-beep, beep-beep-beep-beep-beep of "Jingle Bells" continued to pierce the air. It grated my nerves. My lungs constricted in panic. I fumbled blindly, trying to retrieve my phone before another chorus could assault me. My fingers finally landed on the vibrating, singing banshee posing as a cellular device.

"Yeah?" I croaked. My tongue had the dry sour taste that comes when you know you drank too much. *I swear, I don't remember drinking…*Then again, I didn't remember much of anything. My pounding headache argued there may have been drinking.

"What do you mean, yeah? Where are you, agent?" A valid question, if I knew the answer. I wiggled out from under the table to get better data. And air. I needed fresh air. Badly.

The anger-bear on the other end of the phone was my nemesis, Mike Cassidy. Another word for him might be boss man. Another word for him would be inappropriate, insubordinate, and grounds for termination. I kept that word to myself.

"Where do you think I am?" I snapped back. It felt like I was swimming through a dream. A memory? What's the difference, honestly?

I blinked some more, willing my brain to function. *He sounds grumpy today.* Not that I was much better.

"You're supposed to be at the Cineplex for a staff meeting in an hour!"

There it is.

I was at the movie theater. My brain processor was back online. Let's recap before the spiraling red wheel of death forces me to reboot completely.

Number one. I work for the FBI, and I'm on an undercover mission.

Number two. My plane landed at Seattle International Airport late last night.

Number three. I drove straight north for an hour to get to Skagit Valley.

Number four. I dropped my bags at my best friend Halia's place…and ended up at the theater.

Why did I go to the theater?

"I'm getting to it, man. I'm already there." I struggled to sit up and look around. I really was at the theater. I couldn't remember how. I barely remembered the drive.

I must have rushed right over after Halia's party, or maybe before I even made it to the party? I must have snuck inside before the last showing. There was no other logical explanation for how–or why–I was at the theater.

"Bly, if you fuck this up, you're done," Mike warned.

Such a gentleman. Mike was the clean-cut, no-nonsense kind of guy the FBI traditionally loved to put in positions of power—whether they deserved it or not. He was the type of guy who despised young agents like me because I possessed a particular set of skills he did not. Skills I used to hunt things down. Skills I used to… I'm just playing.

Seriously though, the FBI did not hire USC summa cum laude nerds like me because we're cute. They hired us because we're just this side of hackers ourselves. We understood the digital world. We move within the expansive gateways of information without training wheels. The ones and zeros mean something to us. They mean something to me.

All the weapons, training, and pushups did absolutely nothing against hackers. And it was quickly becoming frighteningly apparent law enforcement, not to mention our laws, were woefully underprepared for the digital age. Catch up, congress. Seriously.

Anyways. Mr. Grouch Monster, Mike Cassidy, was mad because even with my particular set of skills, we were nowhere closer to finding our unsub—that's Fed speak for unknown subject—*Key$troker*. Yes. It was and remains a *very* stupid name. I suppose we can't all be Deep Throat or Jason Bourne.

Like all responsible hackers, this clown shoes was using an online alias. Something they felt captured their essence. Don't ask. I don't know, either. *Key$troker* belonged to a troublesome digital pirate somewhere in the Skagit Valley, nestled in Washington state.

Mike and his Seattle agents *should* have been able to handle *Key$troker* and their shenanigans. Especially with all the Amazons, Googlers, and Softies. Side note: Microsoft has the *worst* nickname in tech if you ask me. My point is, they have plenty of talent in the Pacific Northwest. Plenty of capable people ready and willing to gobble up a good mystery.

But, unlike Mike's male-dominated-middle-age-neckbeard crowd, I fit the skill set *and* the social profile for this particular undercover role—twenty-something, female, computer literate, and, most importantly, passably local. A person on the ground who wouldn't scream FBI when I walked through the door.

Yesterday, I'd been sent to my hometown to do just that.

I hadn't been home in ten years. But sure, let's head home for Christmas. *Surprise! Did you miss me?* Sounds delightful. Yay… Right.

I'd once done hard time working at this theater when I was a teenager in high school. I knew the job, the expectations, even the building inside and out. It should be a total cakewalk.

Although…

Anyone who has ever worked a day in customer service will tell you that was a big fat lie. Customer service will always be one of the most abused industries on earth, even if service is the backbone of most modern economies. No matter how fun working at a movie theater might be, it will always be a public facing service job. Let's just be honest. Customers are assholes. And no, you are *not* always right. In fact, you are most definitely wrong about at least one thing in your argument. And don't get me started on the robots.

End rant.

"I know what's on the line, Mike," I sighed in resignation. The theater would be my second undercover op. My first solo mission. Until recently, I'd been the youngest desk jockey in my division at the ripe old age of twenty-eight. It was hard to be taken seriously when you were a computer nerd with boobs. Every woman everywhere knows exactly what was on the line in this position.

"Good. And it's *sir* to you, agent. Because, unless you want to spend the rest of your life working at that shit-town theater, I suggest you find a solution. Yesterday."

I let the obnoxious Nokia brick drop to the floor the second the connection ended. He knew I'd only been on the ground for less than twenty-four hours. *What a punk.* It was just dumb luck I was already at the theater. I would never have made it on time if someone hadn't stashed me under the coffee table.

Some soulless cretin in corporate decided Christmas Eve would be an *excellent* day to have a staff meeting, rather than *any* other day in December. And, because we can't have nice things in the service industry, the staff meeting was also at 7:30 a.m. My first day on my new-fake-job, and there was a bloody staff meeting. Before sunrise. A guttural growl is how I feel about that.

"Uuuugh!"

At least drunk me was mindful enough to set up my laptop and jack it into the hardwiring in the wall, thank god. *How was drunk me able to get a plugin into the wall?* It didn't matter. I wiggled all the way out from under my iron prison and stretched until my spine popped, settling my meat puppet back over my weary bones with some satisfaction.

"Ow!" I yelped.

A low-hanging garland of Christmas gnomes caught me right in the eye. I hadn't noticed the haphazard decorations strung by Santa's minions in the crushing darkness of the booth. No normal sized person would hang decorations that low. I pressed a palm to my right eye and glared at the festive trolls.

They bobbled indifferently.

I stumbled onward, focusing on the soft green glow of

ones and zeros from my computer. Its rhythmic pulse was far easier on the eyes than the blazing ball of flame posing as a ghost light. Elbows propped on the desk, I shielded my eyes with my hand as I watched code scan and file into folders. The visual scroll was therapeutic and comforting. Something familiar while I pondered how all of this fit together.

Then, I spotted it. An empty bottle of tequila was in the trash beside the work desk. Don't worry, I didn't drink it *all*. I'd have woken up dead. But it was most definitely why I woke up under the godforsaken iron table in a dark corner.

Somewhere between the drive and the empty bottle, I… lost track of everything. *When did I drink tequila?* Was it yesterday? It felt like it may have been yesterday.

My profound sense of déjà vu was interrupted when the overhead lights suddenly blazed to life. Spots of red and orange seared my brain in strange shadows. The projectors shimmered like hulking metal ogres in my blindness.

The managers must have arrived. Their first order of business would be to warm up the building, starting with the projectors. The booth operators would be minutes behind them.

A loud *creak, thunk, thud* echoed down the hallway as a heavy door banged open somewhere in the darkness. My heart leapt to my throat, and I spun around. To my undying relief, whoever entered the projection booth entered by theater six, not by theater three. I exhaled swiftly.

They have not seen me. Not yet.

My vintage Ms. Pacman wristwatch blared a warning. *6:25 a.m. I can make it.* I fumbled to silence it, looking around frantically as I slammed my laptop shut and yanked the cord free from the wall. There wasn't time to worry if my computer had finished any decryption. If I was very, very lucky, I might be able to sneak out of the booth and into the locker rooms without being noticed.

I shoved all of my belongings into my shoulder bag, whipped the strap over my head then bolted for the door. Heavy boots stomped on the linoleum like a heartbeat.

Opening procedures were headed my way.

CHAPTER THREE

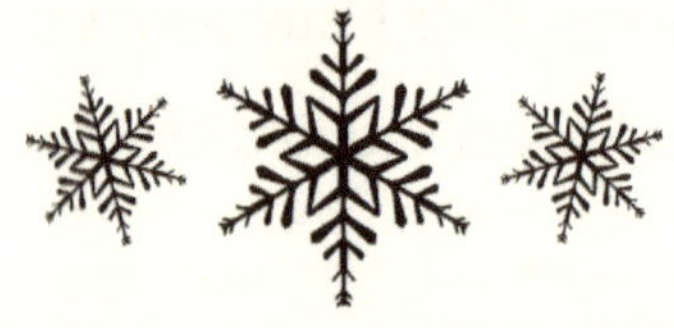

Stink, Stank, Stunk

I can make it.

I quickened my steps, bursting through the door in a rush barreling into an unseen person who bellowed in alarm. I shrieked in reply. We both stumbled backwards in surprise. Shallow gasps burned in my chest, my pulse ricocheting through my veins. It took an insidiously long moment to register that I ran into a person and not a monster.

"You gave me a heart attack!" I wheezed, a hand pressed to my sternum in a futile attempt to calm myself down.

"What are you doing here?" a deep velvety voice asked.

"I was…" Our eyes met. I found myself drawing a blank on things like words, my brain a mash of alphabet soup. Slack-jawed, I gazed upon the most beautiful mortal I'd ever seen.

He wore his night-dark hair combed neatly behind his ears in casual waves. A day-old beard scraped over his marble-cut jawline. His flawless bronze skin positively glowed. Michelangelo himself had chiseled this man's face.

Tailored black slacks and matching gothic black shirt cut neatly across his broad shoulders before tucking into a trim waistband. Corded muscles and solid legs stretched as he stood to his full height, 6'5" at least. His eyes were pools of Cognac that sparked with delight. An amused smile tugged the corners of his mouth. He smelled like orange blossoms and cinnamon. A soothing scent that settled my roiling stomach. I wondered if he would taste the same.

What? Who said that. Oh, wait, it's me.

"Did you get lost?" he asked, head tilted to consider the pitiful creature in front of him.

"I've been here before," I managed in a whiny protest, blinking stupidly at him. "I need…"

I needed to sober the hell up before I made a complete damned fool of myself. I shook my head, attempting to shake my muddled brain back into alignment.

"I'm Malachi," he said, hand extended in greeting.

"Please don't tell the managers," I begged, completely ignoring his proffered hand. "It's my first day. I would really like to not get fired on my first day."

"Alright," his mouth quirked into a wry grin and he tucked his hands into his pockets. "How did you get in the booth?" he pressed again.

"Oh. I worked here ten years ago. As a projectionist."

He remained unconvinced.

"Y'all haven't changed the code."

His eyes tracked to the keypad then back to mine. I really hoped it was the same code. Cause I still have no good reason for how the hell I got into the projection booth in the first place. *Must. Find. Coffee.* I gave him a winning smile, hoping confidence would counter my woke-up-hungover condition, and ducked past him. His gaze lingered, a warm tingle on the base of my neck.

"Thanks for not ratting me out," I saluted before shoving into the women's bathroom.

I hissed at the blinding white lights, shielding my eyes to take a good look in the bathroom mirror. *Why are all the lights in this building so damn bright in the morning?* Inquiring minds must know.

My appearance elicited a sigh of distaste from the depths of my soul. My Celtic skin was sallow in the harsh tungsten light. Yesterday's tattered FBI t-shirt was drunk-girl wrinkled. My green corduroys smelled of stale cheese puffs and disappointment.

I cringed when I considered what Malachi might have thought at the sight of me. Or the smell. Oh no. He smelled like a fresh cup of muddled cider on an autumn morning. I smelled like that afterbirth of a rave concert. *Gross.*

Thank god my past self was mindful enough to tuck fresh clothes into a go-bag along with my computer. I snapped out a *Christmas Things* t-shirt with a glittery graphic garland of *Disney/Stranger Things* ornaments. I didn't remember packing it, but FBI training was always good for one thing: preparedness.

Muscle memory did the rest for me. I plunged my face under the faucet, the icy water sluicing away the last dregs of sleep. Droopy red curls, smeared day-old eyeliner, and faded red lipstick were beaten into submission with paper towels and an iron will. It was a botch job at best, tidying my face and rage brushing my gums until they bled.

Yesterday's clothes were stripped, bagged, and tagged. Standing in my underwear and bra, I cracked my neck just as the door swung open.

"Heavens to Betsy, Zoë!" Bette exclaimed. Bette, short for Bethany, was the most beautiful and vivacious black woman I ever had the pleasure of knowing. It was Bette, more than anyone, who encouraged me to leave this small town after my mother died.

"Life is what you make of it, girl. Your life is waiting for you somewhere else. Go find it," she'd told me after graduation. Bette and my mom had been church friends when I was little. Before everything changed. Bette knew the real me. She had accepted my pathetic plea to have my job back, no questions asked.

"Just come home," she'd told me.

I really loved Bette.

Unfortunately, she was also the infuriating sort of woman who was completely put together at 6:25 a.m. on a holiday, ready for her day. Her hair was perfectly styled, the makeup effortlessly flawless. It was enough to make a grown woman cry.

She took a long hard look at me in my underwear. Comparatively, she wore a well-cut violet blouse over her buxom frame. It shimmered like satin but probably breathed like cotton. Bette was a practical woman. It got hot at the theater.

"Sorry, Mama B," I smiled broadly, unashamed. Modesty and I weren't the best of friends. And, Bette wasn't one to judge. Mostly.

Just seeing her beautiful face again felt like a warm hug. I felt better than I had all morning.

"What are you doing in your skivvies, Zuzu?" she

demanded.

"Just changing before the meeting." The cold cotton t-shirt and clean jeans felt like silk as I pulled them on. I shuddered in pleasure.

Bette eyed me suspiciously, the universal look when mama catches her kid with their hand in the cookie jar. She strode toward me, one fist planted firmly on her hip.

"You been drinking?" She hooked a finger under my chin, forcing eye contact between us. I had the good sense to appear sheepish and felt my cheeks flush with embarrassment.

"Not since last night."

"I should send you home."

Her soulful brown eyes were full of warmth and wisdom. And more than a little bit of judgment. Totally deserved. I gave her my best impression of abject failure, hoping I projected pathetic burnout enough she would take pity on me.

"I suppose that wouldn't be the same kind of punishment as making you work a double shift on Christmas Eve, now would it?" she clucked at me with satisfaction.

I hadn't thought about that. Being sent home on Christmas Eve sounded like Christmas morning. Her smile was smug, sauntering down the row of toilet stalls for her morning business, whistling "Twelve Days of Christmas."

Damn.

For the record, Bette was not usually a villain. Working the Christmas holiday double was the price she had demanded when I called and begged for my job back. She told me I'd better be here at 7:00 a.m. the next day, neglecting to mention the staff meeting. She had me by the ovaries, and she knew it.

I would be working an *entire* double shift.

Double damn.

"And brush your teeth, child," Bette hollered through her closed stall door. "Your breath is foul."

Cheeky old crone.

CHAPTER FOUR

Cup of Cheer

After I put on pants… and brushed my teeth… again… I headed for the lobby to get my bearings. My black Airwalks padded silently over the squishy polyester carpet one only finds in casinos and movie theaters. It always smelled of melted butter, warm bodies, and putrid sugar at the theater. The scent immediately assaulted my system the minute I rounded the corner for the lobby. I braced myself against a wall rather than find out just how hungover I might be.

It sure as hell wasn't cinnamon and orange blossoms.

I sucked in a determined breath of air and gagged on the scent of burnt oil and sugar. If I didn't get real food and caffeine in my system stat, I would be making an unfortunate imitation of Linda Blair. I closed my eyes, focused on the grounding aroma of coffee, and followed my nose.

Like every native Pacific Northwesterner alive, I personally have a one-track mind when it comes to coffee. No, your single venti non-fat Starbucks milkshake does not count. We're a pot a day people. We are coffee snobs. Coffee is the lifeblood which must be consumed before any rational things could happen.

I directed bad thoughts to whoever's idea it was to have a staff meeting on Christmas at the crack of dawn. It would be nice if they at least let us wake up first. Though, I suppose you couldn't exactly shut down a theater for something as trivial as a staff meeting at Christmas time.

The hamster wheel must turn.

Mercifully, Bette always bought the good coffee, local donuts, and fresh bagels for the industrious among us. There was also orange juice to pacify the health conscious crowd. The delicacies were generously laid out on twin folding tables across from theater seven, where the meeting would take place. People were already helping themselves.

I made straight for the caffeine drip, snagging a maple bar and stuffing the donut halfway into my mouth. I began to doctor my coffee. And by doctor, I meant drown the caffeine in sugar and milk. Pros like myself avoided the bottle of powdered shame that some people use for creamer. Bette, the queen that she was, provided us with fresh half-n-half.

Thank you, Bette.

"I take it you like coffee with your cream and sugar," teased a familiar gravelly voice from behind. I choked on the donut in my mouth, half of the sugary pastry falling back to the table. The same tall-dark-and-mysterious man from earlier was grinning at me with his perfect porcelain teeth. I stopped breathing until my brain remembered oxygen was required for life. Forgetting the donut, I sucked in a breath and promptly began coughing like a barking seal.

"Are you okay?" he asked. I sputtered and choked, struggling for air. I managed to swallow, washing down the last chunks of fried dough and sugar with a swig of coffee. I wiped salty stinging tears from my eyes with the back of my hand.

Mystery man soothed my choking with a gentle pat on my back, his brows knit in concern. He was several inches taller than me, bending to examine my face, his eyes sweeping up and down.

My primitive body betrayed me. Blood rushed to my cheeks. My pulse began to thunder in my throat. It had been ages since anyone triggered such a magnetic reaction in me. *Danger, Will Robinson! Danger!*

"Just peachy," I managed to croak out.

His hand lingered delicately on my spine. I gulped, begging my heart to return to normal. If he were some preternatural creature, I'd have been toast. Predators sense these things. Thank the stars, he was just a regular hotblooded male. He sensed none of my roiling emotions.

"Zoë!" Halia shrieked.

Malachi quickly withdrew his hand, sucking away his warmth with him. A flash of guilt washed over me, as though I had been caught playing five minutes in heaven. My system was about to crash from overstimulation.

I stepped on my own foot in an attempt to ground myself. I barely gained my balance as Halia, my best friend since we were eight, threw her arms around me in a crushing embrace.

"I missed you too, Halia," I laughed, fighting a surprise rush of tears. I didn't expect to feel sentimental today. I had not seen her in ten years. She smelled like mangos and vanilla, her favorite lotion. I inhaled deeply, a twinge of longing piercing my heart. Halia smelled like home.

How she managed to pull herself together at this unholy hour of the morning, I'd never know. I was suspicious dark magic may be involved. Halia and Bette may very well be in a coven.

Halia was effortlessly festive in a purple sweater of

dancing gold snowflakes. The bold color set off the lustrous glow of her chestnut skin. Her fawn-like brown eyes were set in the perfect oval of her face. Her black and burgundy hair was pulled between a dozen bands. The effect created a crown weave of silky locks before cascading down her back.

God, she's stunning. It simply wasn't fair how gorgeous my best friend was.

"Morning, Halia," Malachi said, his face brightening at the sight of her.

"I see you've met my roommate, Malachi. Our newly minted manager." Halia smiled at Malachi in a familiar playfulness. I scolded myself for the twinge of jealousy that twisted into my soul. *Remember. Your prime objective is find the unsub, Key$troker. Gather evidence. And go home.* Getting caught in this Malachi's bewitching presence—especially if Halia had already claimed territory—would only end in fireworks and tears.

Not. Enough. Coffee. Do not engage.

"You're a manager?" *Thanks, brain, I thought we agreed not to speak.*

"You asked me not to tell the managers. I didn't." Malachi shrugged. The mischief in his tone set my temper on fire. He let me make that ridiculous show of myself. Twice. I didn't know if I was embarrassed, angry, or both. *Both. Definitely both. Congratulations, brain. We're back.*

"Well, thanks for that," I glowered. Halia raised an eyebrow with a knowing feline smile as she glanced between us.

"See you inside, Zuzu," she gushed, abandoning us to our awkward standoff.

"Your name is Zuzu?" Malachi asked, eyes twinkling. He tilted his head in delighted curiosity.

"Only my mom calls me Zuzu," I waved a hand dismissively, then spotted Halia loitering near the theater door, still watching. "Mom and Yente over there."

He laughed and offered me his hand. "I'm Malachi."

"You said that already," I said, taking his hand. It was warm and strong. A strange familiarity to his grip, like I was still dreaming. *Have we met?* "I'm Zoë."

"Zoë," he said my name quietly, sending a shiver down my spine.

"Shit!" someone shouted, breaking the spell and drawing our attention to the concession stand.

A dark-haired Clark Kent lookalike had knocked his till off the counter, sending loose currency flying. An unremarkable boy around eighteen with forgettable brown eyes and a shy smile rushed to help. The boy dropped a bag of popcorn seeds in the process, spilling kernels everywhere.

Chaos erupted.

"Excuse me," Malachi said with a grimace, marching to rescue his staffers.

Man, I am glad I am not over there this morning. I shuddered and shuffled after Halia to wait for the meeting.

CHAPTER FIVE

Babe's in Toyland

The staff meeting was so mind-numbing and long I blacked out. Can't remember a thing.

I did know I spent a large portion of it glowering at our dark and mysterious overlord, Malachi. Then I scolded myself thoroughly. Uncanny handsome managers would be nothing but trouble. I simply could not have any distractions if I wanted to get out of the theater by New Year's.

Those of us working the morning shift booked it upstairs to change as soon as the meeting ended. The lucky bastards who did not work the matinee, hightailed it out of the building as fast as their feet could carry them before Bette had finished saying,

"That's a wrap."

In the lobby, a gaggle of staff congregated around the manager's station by the time I made it back downstairs. Bette was studying a paper schedule, checking it against faces. It was her best guess which staffer would survive the holiday onslaught in any given position. Today was going to be a shit show no matter what Bette did.

There were three possibilities: concessions to shovel popcorn, usher on the floor to clean popcorn, or in the box office to sell tickets to buy popcorn.

My stomach and I grumbled at the memory of my lost donut and coffee this morning. But popcorn sounded completely unappealing in that moment. I sighed and dug in my pockets, hoping I'd left a Snickers or granola bar. I discovered a half-eaten package of gummy bears and chuckled to myself. Gummy bears made everything better. I popped one in my mouth, patiently waiting for my next instructions.

"Boo!" Halia blurted, gripping my shoulders with both hands. Everyone around us jumped in fright.

"Christ Almighty, Halia!" I shrieked, damn near choking on a gummy bear. I was going down by snack food today. "Was that absolutely necessary?"

"Yes," she answered primly.

Bette gave us both a disapproving look as she called out

placements. "Thor, you're my usher. Check the men's restroom. The janitors have been avoiding it again."

The forgettable young man with the mousy brown hair cringed as she handed him a sheet of paper. It was a list of movies coupled to their start and stop times. He lumbered away, reading the sheet and eyeing the balcony with distaste. *Good luck, buddy.*

"Consider us even, after you bailed on me last night," Halia said, handing me her Salvador Dali's *The Persistence of Memory* tie.

"Appropriate," I said.

"I thought you'd like it," she mused. We'd already changed into the uniform. Halia made flawless work of her own. She was always one of those infuriating women who made anything she wore look better. And I do mean *anything*.

Everyone but managers wore the same thing: white collared shirt, black vest, black slacks, black shoes. The staffer's getting to pick a unique tie was some corporate stooge's idea of individuality. A way to tell the customer, *hey, I'm a person too.* Insert eye roll here.

"It smells like popcorn." I frowned and cringed, slipping the tie over my head.

"Just be grateful you're skipping training since you've been here before. You can do videos later," she whispered.

Yuck. Training videos. Every corporation has them. And we all goof off and catnap through the sham of a liability shield. They only force us to watch the nonsense so they can point and say, *see, we made them watch the videos. They should know better than to do whatever it is we're being sued for. It's the staffer's fault.*

Corporate, please.

"You're welcome." Halia crossed her arms, waiting for me to acknowledge her gift.

"Thank you?" I asked with a tone of ingratitude, popping another candy in my mouth. She rolled her eyes and I ate another gummy bear.

"What are you eating?"

"Gummy bears," I offered her some.

"How old are you?"

"You're never too old for gummy bears," I said cheerfully. She retorted with another eye roll.

"Hey, can I have some?"

It was the Clark Kent guy who had dropped his cash till. Up close, the resemblance to Superman was even more striking with his cobalt eyes, jet-black hair, and comic book chin dimple. Unfortunately, he had a painfully soft voice that did *not* match his exterior. He sounded like a kindergarten teacher who sucked in a helium balloon.

The Almighty lost a bet when they made this one, I mused.

Clark Kent stood uncomfortably close behind us, his muscled arm extended between Halia and me. I noticed he was more George Reeves desperately trying to be Henry Cavil and missing the mark entirely on both. This was the sort of guy who worked out because he *wanted* you to know he was strong. The ugly bulge on his bicep suggested juicing may have been involved.

He wiggled his fingers, his greedy beefy palm open between us. He fully expected to get what he wanted. Not a lot a girl wouldn't do for Superman—just don't let this one talk.

Before I could stop myself, I poured a handful of gummies into his presumptuous little palm.

"Thanks, you're a peach," he cooed. He was far too close for comfort. I suspected he was about to kiss my cheek and leaned away from his twitchy lips. He winked. I nearly growled.

"Pecks! Go drool on someone your own age." Halia smashed his face in a practiced face-palm to shove him back. She's been dodging unwelcome male advances since we were twelve.

"Pecks?" I asked in a whisper.

"Isn't it obvious?" Halia shot him a look to kill. Pecks was completely unfazed by her venomous glare. He blew her a kiss, and she stuck out her tongue at him.

"How old are we?" I teased. She stuck out her tongue at me, and we giggled. Honestly, if you are the age you act, Halia and I were still fifteen and not closing in on thirty.

A door opened on the balcony above. Malachi shoved a cart loaded with metal boxes out of the projection booth. Malachi's doppelgänger balanced the other end, grunting and steadying the tower with one hand. He wore a faded hoodie over an untucked, unbuttoned, and generally disheveled, uniform. Except for the just rolled-out-of-bed part, they looked like brothers.

A buzzing in my head flit around this thought. *Are they brothers?* I gasped when I recognized the second man. *Wes Jones.*

He'd started at the theater the same summer as I had. Which was when I learned we also went to the same high school—go Bulldogs! We were nearly the same age, both juniors heading into senior year. I didn't know him well, but I remembered his extreme dislike of my ex, and by association, me. *Just swell.* I fussed with my tie to give my hands something to do.

"I know you like 'em brooding," Halia interrupted my musings. "But good luck with the Grady Twins."

"I wasn't!" I protested.

I was. I am. Tall dark and brooding was a type, and Halia knew it was mine. Sometimes, it was hers too. Luckily, we never actually crossed into the love triangle because our friendship was always more important to both of us.

"Kimber, Xan, you're in the bar with Halia, tills three and four. Amanda, box," Bette said firmly, another side eye for Halia and I. We were smart enough to cower and huddle closer to keep talking as two blonde girls made their way to concessions.

"You were," Halia whispered, batting away my hands to fix the tie for me. "Besides, the brooding one is mine."

"They're both brooding, in case you hadn't noticed," I laughed.

"Yeah, but the booth troll is all Halia's," Amanda, a pixie-haired girl with fierce brown eyes teased before she flounced into the box office and disappeared from sight.

"Which one's the booth troll?" I asked.

"Wes. He doesn't come down except to refill his soda," Halia explained.

"But does he know the airspeed velocity of an unladen swallow? Is that why you call him a troll? Please tell me that's why you call him a troll."

"African or European?" Halia replied without missing a beat.

"You two are weird," Pecks chirped.

"Yeah, but she's my kind of weird," Halia replied, setting the knot in my Salvador Dali tie with delicate fingers. "Malachi is your kind of weird, in case you're wondering. He transferred from Virginia about six months ago. Something to do with the computers, I think."

"Ladies, please!" Bette snapped.

Halia dipped her head close, choking off a laugh with her hand.

A pit opened in my stomach, my mirth swallowed in its depths. Malachi transferred six months ago. Six months ago, we started seeing the watermark. It could be a coincidence.

*Something to do with computer*s, Halia's voice repeated in my mind. It could be nothing… *Unlikely…*

"Yeah, the Dark Lord is our new drill master," Pecks laughed, leaning into our conversation like a meddling neighbor, an arm draped over each of our shoulders.

Nope, don't punch him, I reminded myself. *Punching civvies is bad.*

"The Dark Lord?" I asked. I supposed Malachi did give off a gothic Egyptian Prince sort of charm.

"Whadda you bet it's his code name, like he's special ops Black Hawk or something?" Pecks whispered in our ears, his whiny little voice ringing like a buzzing electronic.

"Go away, Pecks," Halia batted at him like a fly.

"I hear he served in Nam," Pecks was completely undeterred. "Some regular double-o shit, I'm telling you."

"Black Hawks are helicopters. And, he'd have to be at least seventy to be in that war," I said flatly. Working with civilians was going to take an earth shattering amount of self-control.

"See, now shuddup, Pecks!" Halia pushed him away playfully. *Oh… Oh, I see. Halia has a crush on Superman*, I chuckled. *Helium boy is all yours, Hali. I'll take the Dark Lord, thank you.*

"Greg, concessions," Bette said, louder than was strictly necessary. Pecks sauntered away, unfazed by Bette's tone.

"Zoë, you're my floater today. I'll need you for breaks just about everywhere. Let's start you in concessions," Bette continued.

I had an internal sigh of relief. There was a walk-in freezer behind the bar where one could scream in peace if you needed a minute away from people. I'd be just fine disappearing into its arctic embrace when my anxiety kicked in.

Halia must read minds because she gave me an unexpected hug. It had been far too long since I'd come home. I never did have a great poker face for people who knew me like Halia did. She squeezed my arm again. I leaned my head on her shoulder, tears beading in my eyes.

Maybe that's why this assignment was so hard. These people *knew* me. Undercover with people you know… It just wasn't done, for a reason. They would know who put one of them behind bars. I didn't even want to consider it might be someone I cared about.

"Come on, I need help with theater checks. You take one through five and I'll get the rest," Halia said, pushing me down the hall.

CHAPTER SIX

Stealing Christmas

You would be surprised how often something was "found" in a theater from the night before. Once, it was an actual real live person. At least , I think they were alive. It could have just been a dead body.

The point is one body was all it took for morning checks to become a *priority*. Every. Single. Day. Someone must physically walk through all fourteen auditoriums to make sure there were no surprises.

So, I headed for theater five. It was clear at the tail end of the hallway, right before the glass exit doors. Emergency floodlights burned through the night to help the janitorial staff *see* the goddamn mess customers left behind. Seriously, people. Do you throw the popcorn and soda on the floor at home, then leave it? What's wrong with you?

Four hundred seats were arranged in fifteen stadium rows, making it the largest auditorium in the building. The check sheet waited patiently, mounted at the bottom of the steps near the fire exit.

I took them at an easy gate, stretching my legs. The movement was invigorating, my body finally starting to wake up. I didn't even mind the blinding floodlights.

Mostly.

I stopped at the landing. Black walls stretched 100 feet high and bordered a large silk screen the color of starlight. When the Balrog challenged Gandalf and blew out everyone's hearing four states away, it was the base speakers curtained off beneath the screen in theater five that did it.

This morning that curtain was askew.

A cardboard box of DVDs, shrink-wrapped in glassy plastic, peaked out from under the heavy fabric. *Someone must have been rushing.* The disks were thrown in the box haphazardly, sharp angles jutting into the spines and covers of other DVDs. I grabbed one. A rosy-purple picture of Leonardo DiCaprio and Kate Winslet, poorly Photoshopped over a small boat. *Titanic in 3D,* it read in bold type.

"Seriously?"

I jumped as a loud clang echoed through the auditorium. In the blinding flood lights I could barely see. A dark figure stood ominously next to the projector behind a small window. They were completely shrouded in silhouette. It was impossible to tell who it might be at this distance. Curious about my discovery, I returned my attention to the DVD in my hand. The break I needed and it was only the first day. *Hot damn!* I could call Mike Cassidy tonight and report I found *something*.

The emergency lights suddenly blacked out. Panic surged, and my breath burned in my chest. I could hear nothing but rushing blood in my ears as my pulse raced in the darkness.

"Deep breaths. They're just threading the film. Just getting the auditorium ready for the day," I reassured myself. Wes… or Malachi… or whoever… just happened to kill the lights in the theater… at the exact moment I happened to find a box of contraband. *Just a coincidence.*

I waited for my eyes to adjust, the gentle track lights set into the floors warming to a soft glow and banishing the crushing darkness that blinded me.

The projector stood alone, a shadowy sentinel watching over a sleeping valley of upholstered seating. Whoever had been there was gone. My eyesight and heart rate returned. I took another calming breath before I started walking.

In my right hand, I was still holding my evidence. I weighed my options—go straight to Bette with my discovery or save it for the FBI. If I went to Bette and she knew… I shuddered at the thought. Agent Cassidy was my best option to not get anyone I cared about in trouble without a damned good reason. If I skipped morning checks, I might have just enough time to hide it in my locker. I tucked the DVD into my waistband under my shirt and ran.

I was eager to call Mike and report my discovery. Unfortunately, I had misplaced my phone. It wasn't anywhere in my locker or bag. I would have to retrace my steps. Probably in the projection booth since that was the last time I used it. I filed it away on my to-do list and rushed back to the lobby before anyone noticed I had gone rogue.

…to continue reading

The Night Before Christmas…

pick up your copy wherever books are sold!

books2read.com/TheNightBeforeChristmas

Or visit the author's website

www.eringowrite.com

To get your free copy of the spooky fantasy anthology

"Where the Wind Howls"

Featuring eleven indie authors

MRS. CLAUS' SOFT GINGER COOKIE

Will not cause blackouts. Probably.

✻ 1 C softened butter ✻ 1 C sugar ✻ 1 egg, room temperature ✻ 1/4 C molasses ✻ 2 1/4 C flour ✻ 2 tsp ground ginger ✻ 1 tsp baking soda ✻ 1 tsp ground cinnamon ✻ 1 tsp ground cloves ✻ 1/4 teaspoon salt ✻

Directions: 1) Combine the butter & sugar in a large bowl until creamy. 2) Add egg and molasses and whisk until mixed 3) In a separate bowl, add dry ingredients and mix until well combined. 4) Add dry ingredients to wet ingredients and mix thoroughly. 4) Chill dough for 10 minutes. 5) Preheat oven to 350º while dough chills. 6) Form dough into balls or 1/2" and roll in granulated sugar. 7) place on ungreased baking sheets 2" a part. 8) Bake 10-15 minutes or until edges start to crisp for a soft center. 8) Cool to serve.

✻ Enjoy! ✻

ACKNOWLEDEGMENTS

A sincere and heartfelt thank you to everyone who helped make this, my second novel, possible.

First, my husband Collin. We're here again with a new book and it's largely because your love and support, even through my most challenging health days. You work long hours and still let me bounce ideas off of you. Taking care of me and our girls is a treasure beyond compare. Your faith in my work is why we're here and I can't thank you enough.

Second, my amazing creative team, I salute all that you do. Whitney for helping me polish the drafts, Terry for catching what we missed the first fifteen rounds of editing. Melody and Brittany for helping me cover this story up in a neat little package. Emily for shaping my story into a real book. Meghan for sharing creative ideas and helping me review art work with a skillful eye. Each of you ladies contributed to the final story in your own way.

Third, my new and veteran readers. Believing in a small publisher and independent author is no small thing. Every time you share my story, read my story, or follow along the journey you make the next one possible. A novel is incomplete until a reader picks up the book to imagine. So thank you for finishing this house with me.

Finally, my girls. Ondine and Hermione you bring me such joy. Every day is a wild adventure of imagination, courage, and love. You are where the magic lives.

ABOUT THE AUTHOR

Hey, I'm Erin! I live in Spokane, Washington, with my husband and two kids. I survived stage 2 and stage 3 Breast Cancer while I wrote my first book, *The Night Before Christmas*. My favorite movie is the 1999 *The Mummy*. I'm a mood reader and prefer fantasy or comedy. Once in a while a good thriller, if it has a happy ending. Blue is my favorite color. I write sassy women who are on a journey of self-discovery. My stories tend to be funny, adventurous, and heartfelt.

You are most welcome here.

*Character art by Elizabeth Derry